Rebecca's Hope
By
Kimberly Grist

Copyright © 2018 Kimberly Grist

Published by Forget Me Not Romances (a division of Winged Publications) 2015

All rights reserved. Except for use in any review, the reproduction or utilization of this work in whole or in part in any form by any electronic, mechanical, or other means, now known or hereafter invented, is forbidden without the permission of author or Forget Me Not Romances.

All of the characters and events in this book are fictitious. Any resemblance to actual persons, living or dead, or to actual events is purely coincidental.

ISBN-13: 978-1-946939-99-9
ISBN-10: 1-946939-99-4

Dedication

To my very own Pastor Nelson, my best friend, love of my life and live-in biblical scholar. And to my friends and family who have both inspired and encouraged me, I am immensely grateful for your love and support.

"He has shown you, O man, what is good, and what does the Lord require of you? But to do justly, to love mercy, and to walk humbly with your God."
Micah 6:8

Chapter 1

Dear Papa,
The doctor said I could take the cotton out of my left ear now. But it still sounds like there is something in it…

Rebecca raised her heavy tray above her head to maneuver to the next customer in the crowded diner normally filled with locals. Inhaling the fresh scent of coffee appreciatively, her eyes swept across the room. Rough-sawn plank walls were adorned with horseshoes. A pot belly stove graced the far end. Every bench seat was filled at the large wooden tables. Seemingly overnight, the atmosphere changed from a quiet, small settlement to a railroad town, filled with men who waited to assemble their cattle for shipping while others converged in hopes of meeting with the delayed supply trains.

Her stomach growled as she made her way to the next table. A familiar voice called out,

"Rebecca, what in the world did you let them do to our town?"

Rebecca waived a greeting at her friend, Jonas Weber, and his granddaughter. As she approached their table, Jonas's kind blue eyes crinkled and he smiled at her. He was a handsome man in his late fifties, with dark hair sprinkled with gray. He wore a modest suit with tailored trousers; a sack coat buttoned only at the top to show his vest and watch chain at their best advantage.

Hannah, although small for her age, was an adorable child with long brown hair worn down under a wide-brimmed hat. Rebecca admired the fine details on her outfit. Today, she wore a plaid dress with a full skirt and three rows of blue ribbon trim at the hem.

"Oh Mr. Weber, I am so happy to see you both. How are y'all doing?"

"I thought we might starve before you got here." Jonas's ready smile appeared.

"I know the feeling. Can I bring you both your usual?"

"Yes, and one additional order as well. We are killing some time until my daughter gets here. So, there is no rush."

"Okay, I will let the cook know and then bring you some coffee, while you wait."

While Rebecca hurried to fill orders, she fondly recalled meeting Mr. Weber and Hannah years ago when Dr. Benton introduced them. She offered encouragement to the family, along with advice on how she coped with similar symptoms from asthma. Rebecca rushed toward the kitchen. Sidetracked by her thoughts, she walked straight into the chest of a tall, sturdy cowboy. Strong arms reached out to steady her. Her eyes traveled from a button on his shirt to the bluest eyes she'd ever seen.

She flushed as she stared into his face that seemed to radiate good humor. "I am so sorry."

"Not a problem, Miss. I am afraid it was my fault. I was waiting here, hoping for a chance to speak with you."

Rebecca stared at the man who was at least a foot taller than she, with tan skin, light brown hair streaked with yellow from the sun, and the most perfect smile. "Certainly sir, is something wrong with your order?"

"No, nothing like that. I have been watching for an opportunity all week to speak with you. I know it must seem unsettling for a stranger to want to talk with you privately. Even so, I would find it an honor if you would. We could meet later, wherever you think best."

Rebecca swallowed, casting a quick glance toward the kitchen. Seeing her employer in deep conversation, she seized the moment to satisfy her curiosity. She gazed into the face of this giant cowboy who quickly swept his hat off and placed it over his heart.

Swallowing hard, Rebecca's voice squeaked, "Meet?"

"Yes, ma'am. I know this is unorthodox, but like I said, I've been eating here every day this week. Not only are you about the prettiest thing I have ever seen. You are hardworking and kind. As a matter of fact, I haven't heard you complain once. If you don't mind me saying so, ma'am, there seems to be a lot here to complain about."

Rebecca blushed at his compliments, captivated by his boldness and polite manner. "Although everyone is grateful for the additional business. I believe the short supplies along with the high prices are causing some folks to be what one might call, intolerant. Hopefully, the supply train will come soon, and tempers will settle back to normal."

He quickly glanced back at the dining area filled with mostly loud and dusty cowboys and gave her a wide grin as though she had told an excellent joke. "I suppose you know best about those, intolerant customers of yours. Let me say this; if you were my girl, I would marry you in a minute. I wouldn't want you to work in a place like this, unprotected. I don't mean to imply this is a bad place, mind you. I mean no disrespect, but I've noticed quite a few folks coming and going, some good, but a lot not-so-good. I would be concerned for your well-being."

Rebecca studied the man who began to nervously rub the brim of his hat. She shifted her weight, unsure of his intentions. Thinking it best to make an excuse and return to work, her thoughts were interrupted before she could speak.

"You see that is what I wanted to talk to you about. I would like to court you, ask permission to court you. I wondered if there was someone to ask? That is if you would agree?"

Swallowing hard, she stammered, "Thank you, Mr.— I am sorry I don't even know your name."

Squaring his shoulders, he continued, "Jonathan, Jonathan Pierce. I assure you my intentions are honorable. I am a God-fearing property owner. My family and I own a ranch about fifty miles west of here."

"Thank you, Mr. Pierce. I am honored you would ask to speak with me, especially after such a brief acquaintance."

"Not at all, ma'am. You would make me a happy man if you would agree."

Rebecca shook her head. She'd become immune to the almost daily marriage proposals offered to her while working at the diner, yet she never took one seriously. Due to a shortage of unmarried women in this area, most of the eligible age or sometimes not-so-eligible didn't stay single long. Most, but not her. The one man she wanted to marry was dragging his feet. Rebecca stared into the eyes of the handsome cowboy then blushed when she realized he awaited a response. "I appreciate your offer Mr. Pierce, but I have a beau."

Once again, he gave her a playful grin, displaying dimples on both sides of his mouth. "Might have known. You were too perfect not to be already taken."

Rebecca felt her face redden. *What in the world is wrong with me, reacting like this to a stranger?* "Thank you, Mr. Pierce. Although far from perfect, I am flattered."

Not wavering his steady gaze, he adjusted his hat back on his head. "I plan on being here for the next week or two waiting to ship my cattle. If anything happens, or should you change your mind, I'd be honored if you would let me know."

Really, the man is adorable, Rebecca thought as

she hurried to fill orders and clear tables. Once the rush hour was over, Rebecca placed the closed sign on the door and returned the last of the dishes to the kitchen.

Mrs. Potts approached the work table, with a grin, then elbowed Rebecca good-naturedly. "I was about ready to send out a search party for you. I noticed the tall, good-looking fellow singled you out. What did he want?"

Mrs. Potts possessed an uncanny way of keeping up with all the comings and goings of everyone in the diner, including the ability to listen to different conversations going on at the same time.

Without looking from her work, Rebecca answered. "He wanted to court me."

Mrs. Potts put her hand to her face, dropping her jaw in mock surprise. "Now don't that beat all." Patting Rebecca's hand, she continued. "In all seriousness, as far as appearance goes, you could do a lot worse. From the make of his boots and his hat I would say he could take care of you quite nicely."

I can't believe she didn't mention his smile. Rebecca laughed despite her frustration with another effort of matchmaking from her employer. "You would honestly make a decision based on what you see, and what he is wearing? His hat and boots? From what I remember my father exhibited fine taste in boots. You see where that landed me."

Scuffing a chair to the work table, Mrs. Potts patted Rebecca's hand. "When you have been in business as long as I have, you get a certain feeling about people. Appearance is one thing, and behavior is another. Not only is he handsome but he is respectful and polite. He isn't like some of these men who try to grab you. I also noticed the men he is with are well- mannered."

Stopping her work for a moment, Rebecca stared into her employer's eyes and grinned. "Mrs. Potts, do you think if I possessed two good ears I could keep up with things the same as you?"

Her employer wiped her hands on her apron and wrinkled her nose, ignoring Rebecca's comment. "I expect he did what so many of these fellows want to but can't find the backbone to try. I give him credit for attempting. He did say court, right? That's what courting is, getting to know one another. Besides, I agree with him; things are getting a little too rough here for my liking. Yes, I believe a body could do a lot worse."

Rebecca sighed in frustration, though she felt certain Mrs. Potts meant well. "Why do you suppose a man I have never set eyes on until last week, would intentionally seek me out, while the one person I would like to show me that kind of attention seems disinterested? I wish things were different between Sam and me. However, the past few years have scared him, what with the bad weather and all. He wants to have some money set aside before we set a date."

"If you ask me, Sam seems to be getting along fine. He has a nice home, a profitable business, food to eat. Those two girls of his need a mother, and honestly, I don't like the way he is holding you off. Speaking of such, you won't even have a roof over your head soon. Have you found another place to stay?"

Rebecca pressed her hand to her chest and took in a deep breath, letting it out slowly. *I've all but made myself sick with worry about the possibility of being homeless.* She plastered a smile on her face in order not to worry her employer and friend. "No, nothing permanent. Doc and his wife have offered me the use of their extra room. Mrs. Doc said she could use the company. That gives me a few more days to try and work something out."

Leaning in, her face filled with concern, Mrs. Potts pressed further, "Have you considered staying with your friends, Molly and Adam? At least until things settle down a little in town."

"I don't want them troubling themselves about my problems. They have plenty to worry about already, especially since they lost so much during the last blizzard. Adam is so protective of me, and since he is Sam's older brother, I know it's caused a strain on their relationship and put him in a position where he feels like he needs to choose sides. Not to mention, I don't want to add another mouth to feed at their table."

"Pshaw, no more than you eat, I don't think they would mind. Especially now Molly is in the family way. You could be a big help. What about the lawyer friend of Horace? Have you thought any more about getting his help to go after whatever inheritance your Ma left for you?"

Glancing at the work table, Rebecca stared unseeingly at the stack of dishes. Papa Horace may not have been her actual parent, but he'd loved her like one. He encouraged her to write frequently to her father, sharing with him each academic achievement, her apprenticeship, and every other accomplishment. His death and the discovery the letters written to her father were returned unopened delivered a double tragedy.

A noise startled Rebecca. She realized Mrs. Potts waited for an answer. "Since there was never any money sent to Papa Horace to help with doctor bills, much less to help raise me, I don't know if there is actually an inheritance to be had." *What does money matter when compared to the loss of Papa Horace?*

With a wave of her hand, Mrs. Potts scoffed. "I don't mean to pressure you honey, but I'm worried about the way everything is going in town. Things are getting a little too rambunctious for a young, single miss like you, to my way of thinking."

Looking around the kitchen with a certain amount of pride, Mrs. Potts' mouth tightened, and her shoulders dropped. "The extra work caused from the new business in town has put a strain on all of us. Our stocks are running low, so I am going to have to cut back on our hours at the diner until the supply train gets here."

Rebecca shuddered. Her budget was already stretched thin. *I have been praying for wisdom to know what to do. If Mrs. Potts is about to reduce my hours, I am out of time.* "When do you plan on starting the new hours?"

"I am sorry to spring this on you like this, but honestly Rebecca, based on our supplies, we should start tomorrow."

Lord, I sure wasn't expecting this. Tears sprang

to her eyes. Rebecca blinked rapidly and looked away, so her employer wouldn't see discouragement on her face. "Mrs. Potts, you have always been good to me, and I don't want to give you cause for concern. I do have another option although I have been hesitant about accepting the invitation. I recently became reacquainted through correspondence with my mother's cousin, and she invited me for an extended visit. I have been hesitant to take her up on her offer since we have never met. But with my situation in losing my room at the boarding house, this might be the push I need to go ahead."

Mrs. Potts put her wash towel aside, turned and patted Rebecca's hand again. "These are the kinfolk your Papa Horace said you could trust, right?"

Rebecca took a slow, deep breath as she tried to fight the all too familiar feeling of the tightening of her chest. *Lord, please don't let me be getting sick on top of everything else*, she silently prayed. "What you say is true. The idea makes me feel anxious. You are right though. I will consider more seriously accepting the invitation. In the meantime, I will mention it to Lois. Maybe business has picked up at her dress shop."

Chapter 2

Dear Papa,
I am mad that I can only hear out of one ear. Papa Horace says I would do better to focus on others and not myself. How does one do that?

Rebecca pushed her shoulders back as she approached her friend's dress shop. Muslin, linen, and calico were draped and stacked in the small window display. Rebecca blinked as she entered the shop. As her eyes became adjusted to the room, she took in the whitewashed walls, an undressed mannequin, and mostly empty shelves. *No wonder things are slow.* Although business was excellent for most, the high prices, low stock and the additional unsavory types of men caused the local women to avoid town.

Rebecca grinned at her friend. Lois's curls bounced as she smoothed the fabric. No doubt a few of the men ventured in, attracted by the pretty store owner. Rebecca touched her lip. *If only they had a reason to spend their money.* Putting on a cheery face, she moved closer to Lois.

"Oh Rebecca, I am so glad to see you. I have been bored out of my mind."

"I thought you were going to begin working on making some children's designs to put in the window."

Lois straightened, stiffening her posture. "You and I talked about it. I do think it is a good idea. But with such a low stock of material and very little call for children's clothes, it felt like too great a risk. I don't know what I am going to do if things don't pick up soon."

Rebecca hummed as she walked around the shop, looking for inspiration. "Don't you have any material you could take a chance on? Anything would be better than the stacks of material you have here. Something pretty in the window might spark some interest."

"Look yourself; there is so little to choose from. If I hadn't started working on your ragdoll pattern for the girls' birthday, I wouldn't have done a thing all day."

Rebecca gasped as Lois held up two adorable rag dolls in matching calico dresses. "Oh Lois, these are perfect. The girls are going to love them."

"They did turn out beautifully, didn't they? Thank goodness you brought the feed sacks, or I wouldn't have had the material to use to make their bodies."

Rebecca pulled her eyes away from the dolls and gasped. "Lois, that's it." Excited to put her plan in motion, Rebecca moved the remaining yards of fabric and retrieved several feed sacks from the back room. As she worked, strands of her hair begun to pull away from its bun. *I wish for once my hair would stay put.* She paused to move a lock behind her ear.

"Rebecca, what are you doing? I don't want anyone seeing those feed sacks in here. What would they think?"

Rebecca felt her cheeks grow warm. *I don't want to overstep here, but if I don't do something, I am afraid Lois is going to lose this shop.* "Don't you see? We can make dolls for practically nothing from the feed sacks and some of your remnant material. I know there are plenty of men in town who would love to bring something back to their kinfolk. Maybe we can add a few accessories for the dolls, like a quilt or change of clothes, to see what sells."

Rebecca continued excitedly, working her way around the store, "What do you think about going ahead and putting these dolls in the window as an example? Don't you have a child-size mannequin we can set up as though it's a girl standing with her mother? Then we can figure some way for it to appear as though the child is holding the doll. Let's use the lady figure with something new to match the little girl's dress."

Rebecca cleared the small stacks of material from the window as Lois remained silent, deep in thought.

"The only thing I have close to what you are talking about is the dresses we have been working on for you and Sam's girls."

"That's perfect." While you are at it, is there a way to add the shirt I was making for Sam?"

Lois stopped and took a long look at Rebecca, her mouth turning into a frown. "Now hold on a minute. You want me to use the outfits you have been working on, fretting over, and planning to use for your wedding? You want me to put them out as though they are for sale?"

Rebecca turned her face from Lois. "Sam and I haven't been getting on so good. I think he has changed his mind about the wedding. He has been using me as his babysitter, his housekeeper, and let's not forget my horse is in his barn."

"Now listen here, Rebecca Leah Towns, you know good, and well he would never do that. He is too fine a man. Knowing you like I do, I doubt he ever asked you to do any of those things; you did it because you wanted to help. Although it is a wonderful trait, loving people the way you do, I can see how you could get carried away and take on too much."

Rebecca smiled at the use of the town's nickname for her. Although she was born Rebecca Leah Mueller, she earned the nickname of Towns, by tagging along with her guardian as he went about his business dealings. Because there were so few children in the town, the original settlers adopted her in their hearts and insisted they be called Papa too. The town barber, also the mayor, took the opportunity to make a speech. He declared her the town's child to be affectionately known henceforth as Rebecca Leah Towns.

Lois's eyebrows drew together, and she wagged

her finger at Rebecca. "And if my memory serves me correctly, wasn't it you who suggested he keep your horse? Didn't that help you both, so you wouldn't have to board him at the livery?"

Rebecca nodded. "You are right. But I don't know anything about courting. I've never even had a beau, before Sam. Even so, I do know people are supposed to like one another, to want to spend time with each other. Sam pays Emma to do some housekeeping for him, so on my day off I try to help her with his house cleaning and cooking Molly usually does. But no matter what I do, it doesn't seem to make him happy."

Lois tapped her finger across her cheek. "Rebecca, do you think you might be trying too hard?"

Rebecca sighed. "When Sam's girls get home from school they go to Molly's. I feel like I need to help since Doc told her to stay off her feet. I've been showing them little things they can do throughout the week to keep the house picked up, how to mend, do the wash and such. I know the girls have enjoyed the time I spend with them."

"What about spending time with each other? I thought that was what y'all were doing on your day off at Molly's?"

Chapter 3

Dear Papa,
Aunt Eloise says we should focus on Psalms 46:10, "Be still and know that I am God."
Every time I try to do that I fall asleep…

Rebecca claimed the day she went to visit Molly and Adam was always her favorite time of the week. Molly was like a big sister. Her stepchildren, Seth and Emma, were Rebecca's best friends since she had come to live with her guardians.

Everything about the German style farmhouse was the epitome of home to Rebecca, with its large front porch and twelve-foot ceiling in the center hall which made the most of any breeze. The front rooms were painted in bright turquoise with longleaf pine floors. The kitchen had its own open hearth, and it was Rebecca's favorite place to be. Emma found that funny, noting her favorite room was anywhere but the kitchen.

Molly sat at the table peeling potatoes, as Rebecca shared a recipe. "At suppertime, peel the potatoes and boil until they are tender, drain and set the water aside until it is lukewarm. Next, add one pint of soft yeast to the flour and keep warm. Before you go to bed wet it a little, knead the dough and let it rise. Emma, it would get you out of the kitchen a little quicker."

Emma shook her wooden spoon directly at Rebecca. "The one thing I like about your recipe is the part about getting me out of the kitchen. I absolutely hate everything to do with cooking, especially baking."

Molly smiled as she studied both young women. "For you girls to be such good friends you sure are different. If Rebecca could have her way, she would bake everything into a pie."

"You are not going to get any argument from me, especially when it comes to making the most of leftovers. Besides, everything tastes better in a crust."

Molly rubbed her belly and sighed. "What I wouldn't do for some fried chicken though. If I sit here and watch while you are cooking, I believe you can make a success of it. I wish you would give it a try, Rebecca."

"You better, Rebecca. I've heard it said if you want to find a husband you better know how to fry chicken," Emma joked.

"Well, I guess my husband will have to settle for chicken and dumplings."

Molly laughed so hard she wiped tears from her eyes. "The solution of course is we will have to live close by so Rebecca can do all the baking. I will do the cooking while Emma sticks to gardening."

Rebecca stared into the distance and sighed. "Wouldn't that be wonderful? What I miss the most about living at the boarding house is not only your companionship but the sense of belonging and contentment I have when I am here."

"That settles things. Molly, looks like you and Pa will be stuck with us forever," Emma said.

Reaching for Emma's hand to assist, Molly pulled herself from her chair. "That would suit me and your Pa fine, but something tells me you girls will change your mind and settle in your own homes soon enough."

"Which reminds me, Sam's girls have been awfully quiet. Emma, would you mind going and seeing what they are up to?"

Emma grinned as she took off her apron. "Sure, Rebecca will take it from here while I handle what I do best when I get back, setting the table."

Still amused at their conversation, Rebecca spooned gravy over the roasted meat and placed it back in the oven. She smiled at Molly as she inhaled the aroma with appreciation.

"Rebecca, there is a favor I need to ask. Remember after Horace died how you were a bit melancholy? I kept coming up with things for you to do to keep you busy."

Rebecca stopped her work and took note of Molly's expression. "Yes, I remember. I am thankful for your intervention."

"If I hadn't begged you to help me with Sam's girls I would be at my wit's end. Never in a month of Sundays would I have expected to have such problems with two little girls. If you gave me even a small portion of that kind of trouble, I never would have taken the job Horace offered, to look after you. I don't care how much it paid."

Rebecca giggled, "I do remember how you begged me to teach the girls their letters, so they wouldn't completely terrorize their teacher when they started school. It was the first time I laughed in weeks."

Molly studied Rebecca's reaction as she ran her hands through her hair and twisted it efficiently into a bun. "I don't want you to think I am coming up with a list of things to keep you busy. Although, I really could use help with the girls again, while Sam works on his saddle orders in the evenings. Doc wants me to stay off my feet as much as possible, so by the time I finish supper, Adam rushes me to bed. That leaves the girls with too much time on their hands, and what one doesn't think of, the other will. I was hoping you could come up with something to keep them occupied in the evenings."

Rebecca tapped her finger along her cheek as she considered Molly's request. "I may have the very thing. Lois let me have some more remnant fabric. I was hoping you could help me to lay it out in a way to have enough for both girls to have another new outfit. I could give them something to practice their stitching on while we work on it. We can have them start making things for your babies as well. What do you think?"

Molly laughed. "I think the busier those girls' hands are, the better. But another dress? This will be the third one you've made for them in recent weeks."

Rebecca clapped her hands together. "That reminds me, I finished the pink and blue calico. The girls will look so beautiful in them." Noting the furrowed brow on Emma's face, Rebecca said, "Now don't give me that look. As you well know, the first set was made from feed sacks, and the other two were made from remnant material. Besides, I didn't pay for the fabric. Lois traded it for some of the work I am helping her with at the shop."

Molly rested her clasped fingers over her expanding belly. "Is there no remnant fabric you can pick for yourself?"

"No. Most of the leftover cloth is in small quantities. But you will be happy to know Lois is working on a couple of new blouses for me."

Molly reached for Rebecca's hand. "I wouldn't hurt your feelings for the world. However, what you have on now needs to go straight to the rag bag. Why don't you look in my trunk to see what you can find? There is a blue dress I can't imagine ever being able to fit in again, and it would be too short for Emma. I'll keep an eye on dinner while you go get it."

Rebecca leaned forward and hugged Molly. The door slammed. Emma entered red-faced, followed by the twins who were dripping in mud, discharging a terrible odor.

Rebecca gasped. "Girls, what in the world?"

Emma's lips pressed together, and her nostrils flared. "In case you can't tell from the smell, these young ladies have been in the pig pen."

Rebecca suppressed a laugh. Most days it was difficult to tell one child from the other, but now as they stood covered in mud, their hair plastered to their heads, it was impossible. "Sadie and Grace, your Pa told you not to go in the pig pen. Why would you do such a thing?"

Both girls glanced at the floor and then looked at each other. With a nod, the child she believed was Grace, answered. "The pigs looked lonely. Besides, we didn't exactly go in the pig pen, at least not on purpose."

Do pigs get lonely? Rebecca put her hands on her hips. "Girls, which one of you is going to give me a straight answer?"

"I thought that was pretty straight," the other twin answered.

Rebecca sighed, then changed tactics. "Sadie, you first, start at the beginning and tell me what happened."

Sadie waved her hands expressively. "We've been teaching the pigs tricks. You know like to sit and spin around."

Grace nodded. "Like Pa taught the Mama dog."

Rebecca glanced at Molly, who covered her mouth with her hand. *I obviously have a lot to learn about children and pigs.* "Isn't that disobeying your pa?"

Sadie crossed her arms. "No, we simply call them over, reach in and get one."

Grace smiled widely, the white of her teeth in contrast to the mud on her face. "They like it. That's why they come when we call."

Rebecca's mouth twitched as she extended her

hand in an appeal to Molly.

"Girls, you can discuss this more with your pa. Right now, you best get to the creek and wash. If you hurry, you can be clean as a whistle before dinner. Emma and Rebecca why don t y'all take some clean clothes and go with them? A dip in the creek would be perfect on a hot day like this."

"I think I am going to take you up on your offer of the blue dress," Rebecca said.

Molly's face took on a green hue. She waved one hand over her wrinkled nose. "Please do and be quick about it."

Rebecca grabbed the girls' new dresses, clean undergarments, and towels from the laundry basket, while Emma hurried to get soap and a hairbrush. Once outside they walked in a leisurely pace toward the creek. The girls ran ahead and waded into the water.

Rebecca and Emma followed slowly inching their way into the placid pool. Taking advantage of the opportunity to bathe and relax, they allowed the girls the chance to play before they washed their hair. Rebecca felt clean and fresh as Emma brushed out her wet locks.

"I'll finish up with the twins while you go ahead back to the house. That way you can spend a little time with Sam before dinner."

Chapter 4

Dear Papa,
Papa Horace said I am pretty. Aunt Eloise says pretty is as pretty does. I am confused about that...

Rebecca passed Sam's house, formerly a foreman's cabin made of logs cross-stacked at the corners, with spaces filled with clay and lime mortar. She smiled and took note of the swing on the front porch, where she and Sam spent time talking and getting to know one another. Her mind traveled back, to the first time they met. He'd come to help Adam with the ranch after his wife passed away from diphtheria. Sam was a saddle maker who raised horses and cattle dogs.

Rebecca hesitated, enjoying a slight breeze, a relief from the humidity. Running her hand through her wet hair, she paused and allowed memories to flood her mind. She and Emma had spent all day with the girls, and they were sitting on the porch swing awaiting their father's arrival. Grace and Sadie, dressed in their nightgowns and robes, still smelling of soap, chatted about how their father took time to draw them a story at bedtime. Confused, Rebecca sought clarification. "Do you mean, he reads you a story?"

Captivated by the girls' description, she looked forward to taking part in their bedtime routine during her visits and every Saturday night. Sam's sketches were often beautiful and humorous. Her favorite was one inspired by Grace's bad dream about a wolf at school. Recalling her own nightmares that replayed a traumatic event and injury to her hand, Rebecca shared her concern for Grace with Sam. He responded by telling funny stories about a wolf dressed in overalls. Sam sketched the wolf obediently sitting at his desk, hands up ready to answer the teacher's questions. Both girls laughed hysterically, and there had been no further incidents.

Their friendship blossomed, and on Rebecca's eighteenth birthday, he asked her to marry him.

She'd been sitting on a large boulder in front of the split rail fence, staring at the stunning display of wildflowers and inhaling their sweet scent. She remembered watching a longhorn steer lying in the beautiful pasture, seemingly unaffected by the beauty of the field. "I wonder why the cattle don't eat the bluebonnets?"

Sam paused his sketching and adjusted his hat, taking in the scene. "Don't rightly know. My ma always said it is because they were too pretty to eat. But from the looks of him, I'd say he couldn't care less. Now hold still, I want to make the most of this appealing picture."

Rebecca teased, "You mean of the flowers or the steer laying there?"

Flipping his sketch pad closed, Sam walked to Rebecca and lifted her to the ground. "If you must know Missy, I wasn't paying a bit of attention to anything but you and that sunset." Pausing, he looked to the field. "Although, since you bring it up, he does seem to be a willing model. He sits real still too. I don't believe he's moved a muscle."

Rebecca put her hand on her backside and laughed. "I'm sorry Sam, but that stone was far from comfortable. But I will sit again if you need me to."

Sam put his arm around Rebecca's waist and guided her toward the house, calling for his daughters, "Girls, come on in now, it's time to get ready for bed."

Sam paused and took Rebecca's hand. "Don't worry about sitting again; the time got away from me. I didn't realize I had you up there so long. I wish you'd said something sooner."

Sam leaned closer to Rebecca, his lips parted.

"Pa, make her stop," Grace cried, her squeal interrupting before a much-desired kiss could happen.

"You were the one who wanted me to catch him," Sadie answered.

Rebecca suppressed a giggle behind her hand as she watched Sadie push a large toad toward her sister. Sam chuckled, then called for both girls to calm down. "Sadie, let the toad loose. Grace, for goodness sakes, quit squealing."

"But Pa, I worked so hard to catch him," Sadie

said with a quivering lip.

Sam knelt beside both girls. "Well, I imagine so. That is a mighty fine toad. But I bet he is missing his friends and family about now, don't you? Why don't y'all both go and put him back close to where you found him and then get on to the house. It's about time to get ready for bed."

Sadie's eyebrows drew together, but she nodded in response. "Alright, Pa. Can I pick the story tonight?"

Grace gasped. "Sadie, you know good and well tonight Pa's going to draw us a story about Rebecca when she was little. Ain't that right, Pa?"

"That's right. Now you girls best get to it, or there won't be time for anything but your prayers."

Sam and Rebecca watched the twins hurry to restore the toad and return to the house. Turning toward her, Sam swallowed. His blue eyes widened, as he wrapped his finger around a strand of her hair. The sound of the windmill turning seemed to keep time with the beating of Rebecca's heart as Sam's lips met hers. "I love you," he whispered.

Dropping to his knees, he took her hand. "Will you marry me?"

Gasping, Rebecca covered her hand with her mouth.

Still kneeling, Sam cleared his throat, "So what do you say? You'd make me a happy man if you'd answer, yes."

Rebecca, wide-eyed, nodded in agreement. Her hand shook as Sam placed a ring on her third finger. It was a Georgian style gold ring set with a lovely deep flat red stone. "Oh, Sam; it's beautiful."

Sam stood and reached for Rebecca's left hand. "They say a garnet is the symbol of purity and love."

Rebecca stared into Sam's eyes. "I love you too. I can't wait to become your wife and a mother to your girls."

Now as she approached the barn, Rebecca could hear the squeak and groan of the windmill, the sound reminded her of the promise of a future with Sam. She was disappointed when two months ago, he postponed the wedding, stating the need to earn enough funds to pay his portion of the taxes.

"Rebecca, I love you and want you to be my wife. But I want to have my finances in better shape and have some time to court you before we are married, and you become a full-time wife and mother. You know as well as I do how the droughts, then the blizzards all but destroyed this ranch. But Adam and I have it figured, if all goes as planned the next few months, we should be able to get back on firm footing."

To Rebecca, it sounded like another excuse to avoid something perhaps he really didn't want. *Is he sorry now he asked me to marry him?*

"I'll be working days on the ranch, and afternoons and evenings I'll be focusing on my saddle orders. We can talk about our future after I get things caught up."

Rebecca felt her heart race as she entered the barn and caught sight of Sam. This afternoon, he was in the process of nailing rawhide in place on a saddle. The muscles in his arms flexed as his hammer swung quickly and efficiently. His lips were pressed together in concentration, but the moment he saw her he broke into a smile, displaying a chip of a dimple on the right side of his mouth. "Hello there pretty lady. I was wondering if you were going to stop in to see me today. Is that a new dress?"

Rebecca felt her face blush. "Not new exactly. It is one Molly let me have. I would have been by earlier, but I got sidetracked by a couple of adorable children."

His blue eyes twinkled. "They are adorable alright. But I don't think I like the way this conversation is going. What did they do?"

"Nothing too terrible." Rebecca smiled encouragingly. "Don't worry. They are going to talk to you about it this afternoon."

"Have a seat and forewarn me, while I finish this saddle."

Rebecca approached the railing separating the work area from the barn. As she gathered her skirts, Sam scooped her up and placed her on the rail. His eyebrows rose. "You been sick? It feels like you've lost more weight."

Rebecca blushed. In a previous conversation with Sam about the high prices in town, he misinterpreted something she said and thought she was pressuring him to marry her. She eyed him, wondering how to respond. *Honesty is best*. "I know what you are going to say. But things are expensive in town. Why the price of an apple, for example, is outrageous. I am eating a bit less than I was before, but that can't be helped."

"I thought you ate at the boarding house?"

Rebecca shook her head. "Miss Mabel raised her prices the same as everybody else. I can hardly manage to pay for my room, much less afford to eat there."

Sam gave a half-smile. "I know it's no use me offering you money since you will refuse it. But you need to put your health first, eat more and spend less on other things. Otherwise, a good wind might come along and blow you away."

Rebecca bit her lip and changed the subject. "I thought you wanted to hear about the girls."

Sam's mouth stretched in mock fear. "Not sure want is the word I would use."

Rebecca laughed, then explained the girls' antics with the pigs. "They say they are teaching them tricks."

Sam paused from his work. "Pigs are smart. They like attention too. I knew the girls liked watching them. But I didn't know they were taking them out of the pen. My worry is they will become attached, then get upset when their pet ends up on the breakfast table."

Rebecca nodded. "I guess we have all heard not to name our food. I suppose teaching it tricks would be even worse."

"Did I tell you I caught them keeping one of the chickens in their room? The thing was sleeping with them on their bed."

Rebecca laughed as Sam stepped closer, pulling a piece of paper out of his pocket. Unfolding and smoothing the drawing, he showed her an intricate plan for a saddle.

Rebecca traced the design with her finger. "Oh,

it's going to be beautiful."

He reached for a strand of Rebecca's hair, blowing across her face, then wrapped it around his finger. "It is that."

Rebecca blushed. "Who is it for?"

"I got another visit from your friend, Mr. Weber. He wanted a new saddle for himself and brought me an order for his brother. If things keep going like this, I should be able to pay my part of the taxes, buy supplies and put a little aside. Once, I have things in order; it will be time for me and you to take the next step."

What does he mean exactly? Rebecca was hesitant to pose the question. Finances seemed to be a touchy subject between her and Sam. She avoided his gaze as he reached for her and set her down.

Sam's brow furrowed. "It ought to be about time for dinner. My stomach has been rumbling for an hour in anticipation of some of those biscuits you make. And know this young lady, I am going to watch you like a hawk, to make sure you eat."

Rebecca sighed. "I eat my share."

"I don't know what your share is, but you best double, even triple it."

Sam took his finger and lifted Rebecca's chin to look into her eyes. "I'm not trying to shame you, honey. But you need to take better care of yourself. The dress you have on is pretty, but it is hanging off of you."

Rebecca crossed her arms and glared at Sam. "You've made your point."

Sam exhaled. "Alright, let's drop the subject for now. We have such limited time together I don't want to spend it arguing. Why don't you and I sit down after dinner and look at how you are spending your money. The first thing you should be focusing on is room and board."

Rebecca's hands clenched into fists. "You want to teach me to budget?"

Taking her arm, Sam began leading her toward the house. "I know how smart you are with numbers. But budgeting is hard and takes discipline. You will have to cut out non-essentials, like all those things you keep bringing my girls."

Rebecca pulled her hand from the crook in Sam's arm and faced him squarely. "You are accusing me of being undisciplined? I told you I traded work with Lois for that fabric. Besides, you've never had a problem with me doing things for the girls before. Are you still angry because I talked to my friend about their dresses getting too short?"

Sam looked away, rubbing his chin. "Look, I don't want you worrying about Sadie and Grace. But you are right; I sure don't like you discussing my daughters' needs in public. Let me be the one to worry about them."

Crossing her arms, Rebecca glared at Sam. "As, I recall, you didn't even realize the girls' knees were showing. Would you have me ignore such a thing? Do you want your girls to go around dressed unsuitably?"

Sam placed his hands on his hips. "Now hold on there. Is that not the pot calling the kettle black? Instead of focusing on my kids, you might want to look in the mirror. You are wearing other people's castoffs; your boots have patches over patches, and you are about as thin as a rail."

Rebecca gasped. Her face burned from anger. Turning her back, she walked away as tears rolled down her cheeks.

Sam followed, touching her arm and turning her to him gently. "Rebecca, wait, that came out all wrong. I'm sorry." Reaching into his pocket, he pulled out a handkerchief and gently wiped her tears. "Listen, I haven't said much about my first marriage. But it was an unhappy one. Mostly because we jumped ahead, married too young, and then the girls came along right away. I worked from morning to night, trying to make ends meet, which left her to tend to the girls by herself. When I got home, I tried to take over to help with the girls, but even so, we were both exhausted." Sam blew air into his cheeks and released it slowly.

"I've seen personally how rushing things can ruin a relationship. And when you add money troubles on top of everything else, it will tear a marriage apart. I want to make sure we start out on the right foot, that I can handle the expenses, and my family agrees on how money should be managed." Swallowing hard, Sam looked toward the house. "For now, I think it is best if you concentrate on yourself. I will take care of Sadie and Grace."

Rebecca nodded. *I am not going to stand here and let him see me continue to cry.* Catching sight of the girls as they called out to their pa, she turned and walked in the opposite direction.

Chapter 5

Dear Papa,
I like the stories in the Bible about Moses. Papa Horace says he died before he ever got to Texas…

Adam Brady unbuttoned and rolled up his tight shirt sleeves, freeing the movement of his upper arms. Not one to offer his opinion most of the time, Rebecca was surprised when he had asked to speak with her.

He rubbed his chin and let out a breath before speaking. "Molly and I talked it over. We think you should wait for Sam to make the first move. I personally think you shouldn't go over to his place or do another thing for his ungrateful … for him or his girls. He pays Emma to do work for him. Let her do whatever she and Sam agreed on, and if something doesn't get done, that is fine too."

Rebecca felt her mouth curl upwards. Adam may be Sam's older brother, but she knew that he also had her best interest at heart. Their eyes met for a moment before he leaned back in his rocker. "I remember when you came to live with Horace the second time. It was months before you could have visitors. When they finally asked us to stop by, and I saw the state you were in, it was all I could do not to take matters into my own hands with your father. I credit Pastor Nelson for calming me."

Adam glanced out into the darkness. "He called a special prayer meeting. Men I know had never darkened the door of a church showed up, to ask for God's intervention. It was some of the most heartfelt prayers I have ever heard. I prayed and tried to believe, but I honestly never thought you would make it through the winter. Miraculously, you did and won everyone over with that smile of yours."

Rebecca blinked back tears and swallowed hard. "I never thought about how others suffered because of their concern for me. I have vague memories of struggling to breathe and being rocked in the kitchen, near a kettle of boiling water. And someone was always trying to get me to drink hot tea."

Adam wiped his face with his neck scarf. "God used your circumstance to reacquaint a lot of us with Him. A big part of your recovery had to do with Him sending Molly to nurse you. I will never forget the day I truly noticed her. She was driving you in a pony cart, parading you around town. Later, she held you on her lap and let Emma and Seth take turns driving you. After that, I was smitten."

"I remember when you two got married." Rebecca leaned forward and smiled. "Emma and I were so excited. Molly looked like a princess. On the other hand, poor Seth was miserable because he had a terrible case of poison ivy. I can still picture you both standing in the church listening to the pastor and the advice he gave."

Adam chuckled. "I had forgotten about the poison ivy. He was one miserable fellow. Molly did look beautiful. Every day since I count my blessings she agreed to marry me. As far as the ceremony, I don't recall anything except when he got to the part where we said I do."

Rebecca's smile turned to a frown. "My recollection is the pastor said if you want to know what kind of spouse someone will be, think about how they treat their parents. It worried me since I don't remember much about my mother and what I recall about my father is not good. What kind of wife will I be if my relationship with my father has anything to do with it? Maybe that is why my relationship with Sam is a mess."

Adams' eyes rolled skyward then he gave Rebecca a wink. "There seems to be plenty of blame to go around in that respect. None of us are any good on our own. Which is why it's important to lean on God and allow him to help you to be the person He wants you to be. Even so, you might have hit on something. Maybe it would help you to meet with your father and talk to him about how you feel. It is possible there is more to the situation than we know. I have delayed telling you, but we have received some additional information from your mother's cousin. It was her understanding your father was in communication with you and providing for you financially."

Rebecca's mouth dropped. "You believe that? What about all those letters that were returned to me unopened? If he was interested, the least he could have done was to read them."

"Now hold on. All I am saying is it might be good to get everything out on the table. If nothing else, your pa can apologize for being a heartless low-down son of a ... snake he is."

Adam left his rocker and took a seat next to her. "I'm sorry Rebecca, it is hard for me to hide my animosity for the man. No matter what, none of this is your fault. It is a father's duty to care for his child. I don't want you to get your hopes up. Even so, this seems the appropriate time for you to take the initiative and explore the relationship. If nothing else, it might be a way to allow you to heal and go on."

Rebecca felt her lips quiver, and she wiped her cheeks with both hands to stop the stream of tears from flowing. Adam lit a lantern and approached her with concern. "I know Molly would make you some of that tea she's always encouraging you to drink. How about if I bring you back a cup of cold water instead?"

Adam returned with a drink from the well. Rebecca accepted it gratefully.

"I was afraid I would make a mess of this. Come on now. I can't stand it when you girls cry. It cuts me like a knife to the gut. Which is why I usually keep my mouth shut. Seeing as how your own father was too sorry... I mean is not here to talk things through about decisions you need to make, I felt like I should. There I go again making it worse. Molly would be so much better at this; do you want me to take you to her?"

Embarrassed and not wanting to worry Molly further, Rebecca waived her hand in dismissal. Suppressing a cough, she tried to concentrate on breathing evenly. "No, please don't worry Molly," she choked.

"Don't talk, just listen. I see myself in some of the things Sam is doing. I know something is troubling him. But whatever it is, that's for him to figure out. I don't want you to get caught in the crossfire. What he said was hurtful. He should have expressed it better. Even so, you of all people know how important it is to take proper care so that you can remain in good health. I would never have thought I would say this. Molly and I both agree and think you should accept the offer to visit your mother's cousin."

Pausing for a moment as if to gauge Rebecca's reaction, Adam rubbed his chin before sitting beside her on the step. "You have got to be surprised by that. I am surprised myself."

"We haven't encouraged you to make their acquaintance until now because we were suspicious of the timing of her offer and were uncertain if she could be trusted. Your attorney, Peter has also done some investigating on your behalf. The family has a good reputation, and at this point, I feel confident you will be taken care of and provided for. Besides, I think it will be good to give you and Sam some time away from each other. How is it the old saying goes, absence makes the heart grow fonder?"

Chapter 6

Dear Papa,
Locust came in a cloud and ate everything except for the canned beets. I hate beets too…

Rebecca looked at her feet and sighed. "Lois, I know some of what you are saying is true; when I care about someone, I want to make them happy. But I am making a poor job of it with Sam. I am doing the same thing with you today, aren't I? You never asked for me to charge in here and take control of your business. I am sorry."

Lois placed her arm around Rebecca's shoulders. "Don't be silly. I have asked your opinion about this shop on more than one occasion. You have good ideas and made some valid points. I appreciate your help. You made me realize we need to use what we have."

Rebecca grinned at her friend, "What *we* have?"

Lois gave Rebecca's shoulder a squeeze saying, "You brought the feed sacks, didn't you? We are going to use the dresses you designed, not to mention the doll patterns. I hope you are right because if I don't sell something soon, there won't be enough money to pay rent. Still, do you actually think the men might buy dolls?"

Understanding her friend's concern, she was reminded of a favorite quote of Papa Horace. "Desperate times call for desperate measures." Rebecca smiled at her friend. "I hear some of the men talking about how much they miss their families. Dolls might be the very thing. Have you considered adding some men's shirts as well?"

Lois looked out the window toward the diner and hotel with a frown. "So many men in town and not a woman in sight. My dream was a dress shop, but I see your point. Things are not running in my favor."

Rebecca followed her gaze, touching the window pane. Several businessmen, including her deceased guardian worked together to give the railroad a right of way in hopes of boosting the faltering economy by making their town a water stop and trading post. The plan some called a T-town, was designed and built on one side of the tracks and boasted a post office, blacksmith, general merchandise, barber shop, gristmill, and livery stable. A stockyard had been built a few miles north to create a holding area for cattle and other livestock that would be shipped by rail directly to various meatpacking plants.

Rebecca put on an encouraging smile. "Think of it as a temporary solution, to keep things going until there are more women in town. Do you have any fabric we could use to make more dolls? An infant or handkerchief style with your embroidery skills would have the sweetest little faces. What do we have to lose?"

"There's that *we* again." Lois smiled and brought Rebecca into another warm embrace.

"Whenever I need a good hug, this is definitely the place to come. I was hoping I could take advantage of your good nature and you wouldn't mind me hanging around with you in the afternoons for a week or so?"

Lois blinked back her tears as she regarded her shop. "Actually, I could use the company, and if you can help me implement some of your ideas, maybe we can make a success of this place."

"Thank goodness I haven't succeeded in offending you. My hours have been cut back at the diner, and I could use your advice on what to do next."

Lois gazed at her friend, her eyebrows drawn together, and her lips pressed tight. "I know I am going to be sorry I asked but did you talk to Sam about this?

Rebecca took in a deep breath and sighed. "Whenever the costs of things in town comes up, Sam thinks I'm trying to push him toward marrying. The last time we spoke about my options for living arrangements, the girls interrupted us in their excitement to model their new dresses. When he saw the new outfits, he got mad. Frankly, ever since, I do my best to avoid any subject related to money."

Lois placed her hands on her hips. "Are you talking about the dresses you made from the remnant fabric? Are you telling me, he didn't appreciate the work you put into that?"

Using her hand to cover her laugh, Rebecca said, "Goodness, I have never seen you get riled up so quickly. I can't believe you are making me laugh about this. He doesn't understand why I barter for things like I do. He thinks I usually come out on the short side of the stick."

Lois's mouth dropped open wide. Her normally flawless skin was now blotchy from the top of her face to her neck. "Did you tell him how much that fabric cost me?"

Rebecca raised her hands in surrender. "Hold on now, you are preaching to the converted. I told you he doesn't understand the value of my bartering. Now, if he was to do a job for a tool or a side of meat that would be another thing. But mainly I think he was embarrassed I felt the need to provide for his girls."

Lois frowned. "I know you mentioned he'd been real bad-tempered lately. Still, I would never guess Sam would react like that. Why you only have the nicest things to say about those girls and what a good father he is. My mother used to tell me it was a mystery the way men think."

As her thoughts turned to her problems with Sam, Rebecca sobered. "It makes me feel a little better talking about it. But things went from bad to worse. He as much as told me not to worry about his kids needing clothes when I was as thin as a rail and wearing other people's castoffs."

Rebecca stared out the window and swallowed hard before continuing. "The thing was, Emma had done my hair, and I was wearing a dress of Molly's. She'd told me how pretty it looked on me."

Lois patted Rebecca's shoulder. "How awful. I would like to throttle the man. You may be a little thin right now, but you are beautiful inside and out. I don't suppose you reminded him you were here in town working yourself to death for a roof over your head, and none of us locals can afford to actually eat in town, too?"

Rebecca's lip quivered. "I didn't want him to see me continue to cry, so I went for a walk. I never could hide anything from Molly and didn't want to upset her. But when I got back to the house, she knew everything and tried to pass it off saying all couples had disagreements. She told a funny story about an argument she and Adam had right after they were married. In retaliation, Molly purposely put too much cayenne pepper in his chili. Adam recalled that he never spoke a word and ate it, all the while the sweat was breaking out all over his face and neck. I could never imagine Molly doing something like that. She had us all laughing."

"Later, Adam asked me to join him on the porch after supper. He wanted to speak with me."

Lois leaned closer. "Haven't you always said he was almost asleep before y'all cleared the table?"

Noticing the look of dismay on her face, Rebecca nodded. "Adam usually lets Emma do his talking for him when it comes to most things—especially as it relates to me. But he and I had a long talk. He thinks I should accept my cousin's offer and go for a visit."

Chapter 7

Dear Papa,
Do you think John the Baptist really ate locust? I find that to be a disgusting thought…

"Doc, what's the verdict?" Jonas Weber asked Dr. Benton as his daughter and granddaughter came out of the examining room.

Mary pressed her finger to her mouth to silence her father regarding her daughter's prognosis until they were out of earshot. "Now Papa, you have seen yourself how healthy Hannah has been. Do you need to ask?"

Jonas met his daughter's gaze and gave a curt nod.

"We are going to the dress shop. Come and find us when you are done."

Mary clasped Hannah's hand as her daughter skipped happily across the street. Pointing at the window, she said, "Mama look, it's Rebecca."

Mary met her daughter's smile with one of her

own. "It sure is, why don't we see what she is up to?"

~

Lois and Rebecca arranged the newly-dressed mannequins in the window to appear as mother and daughter, placing the ragdoll as if the child held it.

"We are getting interest already." Rebecca inclined her head toward the glass and the approach of Mary and Hannah Hood.

Lois stopped her work to welcome her customers into the shop. "Hello ladies, it is so nice to see you."

Mary waved her hand toward the window. "I saw y'all working on the display when Hannah and I were walking to her doctor's appointment. Excellent job. It looks like some of the shops I've seen in the larger cities."

If that isn't a gift straight from heaven, Rebecca thought as she stepped back from the window. Mary Hood was one of Lois's few repeat clients who actually paid in cash. She was a tough customer and demanded quality, but when she found it, she was not one to hesitate or quibble over price. *Thank you, Lord.*

Lois tidied her hair. "Good afternoon, I am so happy to see you. Don't you both look beautiful."

Hannah spun in a circle in front of Rebecca. "This is the dress, Miss Lois made me."

Rebecca smiled in response to the young girl's liveliness. "It is beautiful, almost as pretty as its owner."

Mary beamed, as she reached to smooth her daughter's dress. "We have had so many compliments on it. I was hoping to have another made. The mother and daughter set in the window seem perfect. Could we try them on?"

Rebecca noted Lois's hesitation. She bit her lip briefly before forcing her mouth into a smile and moved toward the window. "Let me get them for you."

Hannah bounced up and down on one foot in excitement. "Look, Mama, the dolly has on the same dress."

"You ladies have been hard at work. How resourceful to add the ragdoll."

"The designs were Rebecca's," Lois stated proudly.

Mary glanced up in surprise. "I have seen the evidence of Lois's talent, though I had no idea you designed too, Rebecca."

Rebecca studied Mary's expression to determine her sincerity. Feeling a little shy about her work she stated, "It's not something I typically do. But I have been frustrated with the practicality of some of the current styles and wanted to try my hand at something pretty, yet simple. The dolls are patterned after one my mother made for me when I was little."

Mary held the dress to her chest appreciatively, "I say you have more than achieved your goal. This is lovely. I can't wait to try it on." She turned toward Lois. "I also wanted to speak to you about ordering several dresses for Hannah. She seems to be going through a growth spurt."

Lois's eyes sparkled in excitement. "I'll get my measuring tape."

Smiling encouragingly to her daughter, Mary said, "Hannah, go with Miss Lois, I want to speak with Rebecca a moment."

Rebecca felt her breath catch in her chest as she watched Hannah still carrying the ragdoll walk with Lois toward the back of the shop. It was unusual for Mary to contrive a way to speak with her alone. Watching Hannah now, Rebecca thought her health improvement was astounding as far as she could tell. "Is everything alright?"

Mary reached for Rebecca's hand. "Oh, yes. I am sorry if I gave you cause for concern. I am frustrated with my father's attitude more than anything. He is a wonderful man, but he likes to run his family the same way he runs his business. He is with Dr. Benton now trying to wrangle a cure out of him."

Rebecca laughed. "I can see him doing that. But poor Doc. You left him there alone with your father to fend for himself?"

Mary gave a half smile. "We are honest with Hannah about her condition, but I didn't want to expose her to Papa's rant. He believes God is going to cure her and sees Dr. Benton as the means to get it done. I do believe God can heal her, but even if he doesn't, I am so thankful you helped me to understand the best thing I can do is to learn how to manage her asthma."

Rebecca embraced Mary as she blinked back tears. *What would it be like to have a father like that?* "He may be frustrating, but he loves you and wants the best for you and Hannah."

Mary looked at her daughter who was chatting

happily with Lois. "Yes, I know what you say is true."

Taking a ragged breath, Mary continued. "I can't thank you enough for the encouragement you have given me. My daughter's diagnosis has brought me to my knees on many an occasion. When we received the recommendation of Dr. Benton then ultimately met you, it was a godsend."

Mary wiped her tears with a dainty handkerchief. "When I am discouraged, I only have to think about how you haven't let asthma hinder your enjoyment of life. You have given us hope. You are smart, energetic, talented and living independently. There is no reason to think Hannah won't do the same."

Mary stifled a gasp. Rebecca turned toward Hannah, who now had Lois pulling multiple samples of fabric. "Look, Mama. Don't you think Dolly and me will look nice in this?"

Rebecca nodded in satisfaction. "She is definitely a force to be reckoned with."

Chapter 8

Dear Papa,
Yesterday was my first day at school. Papa Horace said it would be my last…

Having worked for the last two days in silence except for a few grunts and muttered words, Seth stared straight ahead to avoid the angry scowl he anticipated from Sam. He cleared his throat. "Do you want to talk about it?"

"I don't see this is any of your business," Sam snapped.

Letting out a breath, Seth replied, "Fair enough." It's not like I could have helped anyway. After all, what kind of experience do I have with women?" *At least he'd made an effort.*

Hours went by in silence as they rode along the fence line stopping to make any needed repairs. At last, Sam broke the silence. "Listen. I'm sorry to have talked to you like that. I realize you were trying to help. I don't know what's gotten into me lately."

They were quiet again as they got back into their saddles. Seth watched Sam remove his hat and wipe the sweat from his forehead. "Everyone warned me not to get married the first time. I was about your age, went ahead against my parent's wishes, ignored my friend's warnings. It turned out they were right. I was in love with a dream, a fantasy, and except for the love we shared for the girls, it got to the point we could barely tolerate one another. I love Rebecca, but at the same time, I sure don't want to spend the rest of my life arguing about money or playing second fiddle again."

Confused, Seth stared over his shoulder toward Sam. "Rebecca is sensible, thrifty too. She wouldn't have been able to make it on her own for so long if she wasn't. I feel certain you two can work that out. But second fiddle to who? The girls?"

Sam muttered under his breath before answering. "Heck no. I appreciate what Rebecca does for the girls, although I think she spoils them. I'm talking about all those fellows in town always hovering around her." Clearing his throat, he said, "I think it is a matter of time before she throws me over for one of them. Figure, she'll be better off too."

Seth cocked his head in the direction of Sam. "As long as she works in town at the diner, all the hovering will continue. With so few single women in these parts; I don't doubt Rebecca gets offers coming and going. Still, she doesn't take those fellows seriously. From what I know she never even considered allowing someone to court her before she said yes, to you."

Sam rubbed the back of his neck. "That is not what I hear. You can't tell me you haven't heard the same thing. Seems like every time someone comes back from town they have a new story to tell."

Seth gritted his teeth, "Who is saying what, to whom, exactly? If I find out who is saying anything against her, you better believe I won't put up with it for a minute."

Shaking his head in dismay, Sam grumbled. "Which reminds me of another thing. There isn't a person in town who would believe Rebecca would do anything wrong. She's got every man wrapped around her finger. Before you get all riled up, I'm not saying she has loose morals. Still, I know for a fact she's been stepping out on me with Doc's son. What's his name, Benji or something?"

Seth chuckled but tried to cover it up with a cough when he saw the sincerity on Sam's face. "Oh, come on, this is a joke. You can't' be serious, you mean B.J.? Doc's son, B.J. Benton? You are pulling my leg. That is hysterical. You had me going there for a minute."

Seth's jaw dropped when he saw the fury on Sam's face. "Wait a minute. You aren't kidding?"

"I don't see anything funny about it." Sam's jaw clenched. "Every time he is in town he calls on her. I have seen him myself picking her up at Adam's and taking her back to town."

"Sometimes I forget you haven't lived around here all your life, like the rest of us." Seth stroked his chin in contemplation. "B.J. is a nice guy once you get to know him. Real smart, like Rebecca, but at the same time, different. It's almost like he thinks in a unique way, always asking questions, wanting to know, What if? I'm surprised she never told you anything about him."

Sam snarled. "She mentioned him a time or two. Said y'all had all been good friends since you were kids."

Smiling now, Seth leaned back into his saddle as he reflected. "Growing up we always liked it when he would ask questions in school because if he could get the teacher off track, she would forget to give us homework. But B.J. and Rebecca—" Seth shook his head. "I can tell you right now; you are wrong about that." Seth chuckled again.

Sam's eyebrows narrowed. "I don't find the humor in any of this. He comes from money, is all right looking, has a good education. He sure pays attention to her anytime he is in town. Recently, I found out he writes her letters and she writes back."

"True enough," Seth agreed still chuckling.

"Seth, you are starting to make me angry. What is so funny?"

"For it to make sense, I would need to go back a ways."

Only the sounds of the horses trotting along were heard as they headed home. Seth lifted his hat briefly, taking advantage of a slight breeze as he thought. "When Rebecca came back to stay with Uncle Horace, she was so sick; it was months before they let her out of bed. Because she had problems with headaches and dizziness, it was years before they even let her go to church."

"Rebecca loved being around the other kids, but me, Emma and B.J. were about her only friends allowed to visit. She and I would play checkers, but since Rebecca could read almost anything, B.J. would bring medical journals over for her to read out loud. Later, he would have her quiz him on things. It was years before Molly finally talked everyone into letting Rebecca have a trial period at school. We were all excited about the idea. I told Pa, we would take good care of her. None of us had any idea what B.J. planned."

Sam stared at Seth with a troubled frown. "Go on."

Seth met Sam's gaze. "Thinking back now, B.J. would get us to spin around to see if we would get dizzy and to see how long it would last. Afterward, he would scribble his findings in a notebook."

"On her first day at school, everything started out fine. But at recess B.J. headed straight toward Rebecca. Before any of us could do anything, he grabbed her around the waist and began spinning her. She screamed, but he wouldn't stop. Told her it was for her own good."

Avoiding eye contact, Seth swallowed hard before he continued. "I was stunned. I am ashamed to say it was almost as though I was paralyzed and couldn't move. I saw Emma running toward them yelling. From out of nowhere Brian Scott pulled Rebecca away from B.J. and punched him in the nose."

"Rebecca started vomiting. The teacher was yelling, the girls were screaming, and the boys were cheering Brian on. It was pure chaos. The teacher called Brian off, telling him she needed his help getting Rebecca to the doctor. B.J. got up, still pinching his bloody nose. He started yelling orders. I imagine you can guess what happened next. Brian punched him again."

Closing his eyes, Seth was quiet for a moment as the memories replayed in his mind. "The next thing I knew Brian scooped her up and headed for Doc's office. Everything happened so fast. Still, I don't think I budged one inch. All I could think about was Rebecca was going to die, and Pa was going to kill me for letting it happen."

Still seeing a puzzled expression on Sam's face, Seth explained, "Not having known Rebecca when she was little, it is probably hard for you to comprehend how sickly she was. From that one incident alone, it took her about a week to recover. Even though she didn't seem any worse for wear, Uncle Horace told us she wouldn't be going back to school."

"Dr. Benton came over with B.J. to apologize and explained the reason he spun Rebecca around was he thought that would cure her dizzy spells." Seth burst out in a full belly laugh saying. "B.J. has been trying to make it up to her since."

Taking note of Sam's narrowed eyes and mouth still formed in a thin line, Seth apologized. Wiping the tears from his eyes, he said, "I am sorry for laughing. It sure wasn't funny at the time. You see B.J. always wanted to be a doctor like his father. Growing up around Rebecca, seeing what all she went through, he wants to specialize in illness like hers. That is why they write. He asks her questions from her point of view. Now don't get me wrong, I know he loves her but not any more than the rest of us do. He wants to invent the cure for her condition. I suppose he still wants to make it up to her too."

"More to your point, I heard Rebecca tell him one time she could never marry him because she was sure if they ever had an argument he would start spinning her around," Seth said. We all laughed about it, even B.J." Shaking his head, Seth chuckled again. "He told me himself he has a girl now back east where he is going to that fancy school of his. So, you are way off on your assessment of their relationship."

Sam muttered under his breath. "Which explains two things, her relationship with Benji, I mean B.J., and why she seems so enamored with Brian Scott. Based on what you said, I can see why she would admire him. She sure makes it a point to be sitting on the front porch whenever he is at Adam's."

Seth broke unashamedly into a full belly laugh. "I never figured you as the jealous type."

Sam's nostrils flared. "Once again, I don't find any of this funny."

"Listen, they love each other, only not in the way you are thinking. It may seem strange to you, but there is a strong bond between all of us. But I can guarantee you this; when Rebecca sees Brian, she views him not only as a friend but Emma's beau. She loves Emma more than anything. Rebecca would never allow herself to think of him romantically."

Breaking out into another chuckle, he continued. "Another thing, about being out on the porch with Brian. Pa asked Rebecca and me to make sure one of us was out there to chaperone when he called on

Emma. He tried to sit with us a couple of times and was asleep in no time at all."

Rubbing his ribs, Seth continued to chuckle as they made their way home. "I am afraid you have been working on some poor assumptions."

Sam pinched the bridge of his nose. "I've made a mess of things for sure. What's worse is, I don't know how to go about making things right."

Successful this time in suppressing a laugh, Seth added, "Knowing Rebecca like I do, she will forgive you, but she might not forget. You can ask B.J. about that."

"I'm not asking Doctor Benji nothing. You can take that to the bank," Sam replied with a frown and determined look on his face.

Chapter 9

Dear Papa,
Papa Horace says sheep are about as advantageous as locust…

"Emma, when did you say Pa and Seth will be home?" Sam's daughter Grace asked.

"It could be as early as this time tomorrow. Why don't you girls finish up whatever it is you are working on and let's get ready for bed."

Sadie nudged her sister Grace, pointing her head toward her Aunt Emma. "I think we need to tell her."

"Tell me what?" What are you two girls up to this time?"

"Tattletale," Grace whispered to her sister as Sadie retaliated by sticking out her tongue.

"Alright now, I don't like the sound of this. Out with it. What exactly do you need to tell me?"

Staring at each other intently and seeming to understand in a language only twins can comprehend, Grace, bobbed her head and said, "Sadie will tell you."

Sadie crossed her arms across her chest and sighed. "Me and Grace have been figuring, and we talked to our friends at school about it, and we have a plan."

With a sigh of relief, Emma waited as the girls looked back and forth to each other. Surely this can't be too bad, she thought. "Alright, so you and your friends have a plan. Tell me about it."

Grace's cheeks took on a pink tint typical of when she got ready to speak. "Remember the other day when Pa made Rebecca cry? We were real mad, cause we love Rebecca and we want her to be our ma." Crossing her arms across her chest, she cocked her head toward Sadie, silently encouraging her to proceed.

Confidently Sadie continued, "Seeing as how Pa don't want her, we figured to find somebody else around here for her to marry."

Grace bobbed her head up and down in agreement. "That way she can still live close by, and we can visit. So, we asked Mary Ellen to get her Pa to put a notice in the paper."

Emma gasped, as Sadie continued. "We asked Ruth to ask her Pa to pray for her and to put her on the prayer list at church. Kate is going to talk to her pa. He don't have a wife either and is rich too."

Emma placed her hand against her chest as she took in a deep breath, afraid of what the twins might say next.

"And in case that don't work out, Helen's uncle is not married. He is real nice, and if she marries him, she can still be close by," Grace added.

"The only reason you want her to marry him is because Helen is your best friend," Sadie cried as she poked her sister in the chest.

Grace poked back in retaliation with a little more force. "She is your friend too, isn't she?"

"I want her to marry Kate's pa because he is rich, and she will get to live in town. Then we can go see her at her new house." Sadie pushed her face nose to nose with her sister. "Plus, Kate says her pa lets her have candy whenever she wants. That way when we visit her we can have candy too."

"My word, girls, oh my goodness." Emma closed her eyes and placed her hands to her face. Afraid of what the answer would be, she asked," Tell me this, when were your friends going to talk to their fathers?"

Sadie looked at her cousin in surprise. "They already did."

Emma's face grew pale as she sunk into the kitchen chair. "Lord help me, Jesus. Girls, tell me that isn't so."

Chapter 10

Dear Papa,
The weather here is hot, and it hasn't rained in a long time. Sometimes at night, I have bad dreams. When I wake up, Aunt Eloise makes me drink sage tea. I do not like tea...

The Reverend Zachary Nelson walked back and forth in his parlor, preparing for his sermon, but the conversation he'd had with his daughter yesterday, brought a smile to his face. "How is it girls so small could cause such a fuss?"

Martha Nelson found little to laugh at regarding the situation. "Meddling is a problem we are all too familiar with, but our daughter and her friends? They are the sweetest, most angelic little girls. Who would imagine they could think of such a thing?"

"Very enterprising, little angels it would seem," he agreed as he read the advertisement and shouted with laughter.

Wanted: Husband for Rebecca Towns Mueller

Must be handsome, nice, like children, and live within walking distance of Carrie Town Texas School.

"Zachary, I don't know how you can find the humor in this, Rebecca is going to be so embarrassed."

Reverend Zachary Nelson stopped, considering his wife's statement before responding. "She is more sensible than you give her credit for. Besides, Rebecca knows these girls and loves them. I believe she will find amusement in it, especially after she sees the ad they wanted to place. It could have been much worse."

"Thank goodness it didn't get printed in the paper. Poor Rebecca." Martha pressed her hand on her husband's arm. "Zachary, if she hasn't got wind of anything yet, I want you to be the one to let her know what happened."

"Once again, I am fortunate to have married a wise woman like yourself. You keep me focused for sure. Let us hope, in the future; your daughter takes after you in that regard. My sermon preparation is stalled for now, since this situation has me distracted. It will be a good time for me to take a break."

With a stoic face, he turned to his wife. "Pray I handle this in the best way and most of all that I maintain self-control." Leaning forward, with a mischievous grin, he kissed his wife goodbye.

Martha walked with her husband to the door and pressed her hand on his arm, "Zachary, please, whatever you do, do not laugh."

Although he'd made great strides having been

married these many years, in his role of pastor, he still had problems at times understanding women and their emotions. Was he making too light of this? Would Rebecca view this as children who loved her trying to make her life better? He had to agree his wife was right. She most probably would be embarrassed. Not for the first time this week he gave a silent prayer, thanking the Lord for providing him with his wife. "*Lord, she sees things I don't. Please give me wisdom as I proceed.*"

Agreeing he would need to continue with caution regarding Rebecca's feelings he closed the front door. Placing his hat on his head, he paused. A faint sound came from the other side. For a moment he supposed he heard laughter… No, impossible, he thought to himself as he hurried on his way.

Chapter 11

Dear Papa,
The teacher came to the house and gave me my final exam. She said I was the youngest student she ever had to pass the 8th grade. Papa Horace said I could attend graduation with the other students. Please come...

Almost miraculously one of the much-anticipated supply trains came through and delivered the new fabric Lois had invested in, providing a much-needed employment opportunity for Rebecca.

The bell on the door over the dress shop rang, announcing Rebecca's arrival. Lois and Reverend Nelson were engrossed in deep conversation but looked up and simultaneously said, "Good morning."

Rebecca paused in surprise at the hearty greeting. "What a nice welcome and good morning to you."

Walking to the back room to hang up her

bonnet, Rebecca paused to speak to Lois. "I wanted to remind you I have an appointment to meet Peter this morning. I will need to leave around 10, but I should be back sometime this afternoon to help."

Rebecca stole another glance at the pastor, who was intently examining the new fabrics.

Pastor Nelson looked at Rebecca and tugged on his collar. "I was hoping to pick up something for Martha. Perhaps, you could help me decide?"

Rebecca walked closer, fingering the fabric. "What you have in your hand is very nice."

Seeming confused by her answer, he glanced at Lois who took the opportunity to intervene. "Excellent choice, Pastor. Rebecca, why don't you and Pastor Nelson come to the back and have a muffin? It's a new recipe. I would love for you to tell me what you think."

Lois took the fabric from the reverend's hands, then placed one arm through his and the other through Rebecca's and led them to her makeshift kitchen.

The three crowded around her small table as Lois poured coffee and offered each a muffin. "Rebecca, you have seen for yourself how mischievous Sam's girls can be. We need to talk to you about something. Hopefully, after you have a moment to think about it, you will be able to appreciate it."

Rebecca eyed her friend suspiciously. *What could the girls have done that Lois would be aware of?*

Pastor Nelson cleared his throat, as he glanced at Lois. "Well put, Sister Lois, and let me add it is not only Sam's girls who have been up to mischief but my daughter, the bank owner's daughter and much to his chagrin, the newspaper editor's daughter, Mary Ellen. In a nutshell Rebecca, they have been at work trying to find you a husband."

Recognizing the girls were students in her Sunday School Class, Rebecca's jaw dropped. *A husband? But what about Sam? She wasn't ready to give up on him yet.* "What exactly have the girls been up to this time?"

Lois patted Rebecca's hand. "All the girls enjoy spending time with you. They were afraid if you didn't marry Sam, you would marry someone else and move away."

Pastor Nelson pulled on his collar. "The fact of the matter is they were so concerned about the situation they wrote an advertisement on your behalf for a husband."

Placing her hands on her flaming cheeks, Rebecca shook her head, "An advertisement?" She took in a deep breath, exhaling slowly. "Why, except for Mary Ellen, most of those girls are barely reading themselves."

Rebecca felt her chest tighten. Sadie and Grace were undoubtedly mischievous enough to attempt to maneuver such a thing and who better to help them but Mary Ellen. But advertisements cost money. They certainly would not have the means to pay for such a thing. Suddenly the image of the banker's daughter, Kate came to mind. Rebecca closed her eyes, took a deep breath and with tight lips, asked, "Did the ad already run in the paper?"

Pastor Nelson rubbed his forehead. "No, it

wasn't published in the paper. The girls hand delivered them."

Chapter 12

Dear Papa,
Papa Horace says I must pick a vocation. I think I would like to be a circuit preacher…

Rebecca arrived at the law office a little breathless, having tried to match the long strides of Pastor Nelson. "Thank you again for coming with me. Are you sure this isn't an inconvenience?"

Zachary Nelson gave a curt nod. "Not at all. I know how important this is to you. I am happy to offer whatever support I can give."

Peter Marks Jr. walked into the room, offering a quick handshake to Pastor Nelson and a tight smile to Rebecca. "Take a seat and let's review your options."

Looking the important figure in his dark brown, striped, three-piece suit, Peter leaned against the front of his desk. "I haven't wanted to update you until my investigation was complete, though at this point I believe it is best. According to his attorney, your father has been paying for your education and sending support payments for years."

Peter's lips curled slightly. "You are currently enrolled in a costly finishing school, I might add. The lawyer claims he received letters from an administrator at the school giving him updates on your progress. Apparently, you are terrible at arithmetic. What tommyrot."

Pastor Nelson bristled. "Of course, you advised him his information was incorrect."

Taking the chair next to Rebecca, he gave a brief nod at the pastor and continued. "Supposedly, there are records of financial payments, doctor bills, etc. If Horace was anything, he was thorough. Therefore, we have the records necessary to debunk this, which includes your birth and baptism record, custody documentation and medical records, not to mention years of correspondence returned unopened."

Peter's back stiffened as he paused. "Forgive me, that was insensitive."

Standing again, he took a few steps across the room before returning to face Rebecca. "Most of your childhood was spent right here in this office studying along with me. Consequently, I know you have more than an inkling about what will be involved in court. I don't want to see you hurt, but at the same time, I can see where it might be timely from your perspective to retrieve the items your mother left you."

Picking up a copy of the will, he examined it briefly. Then, with a shake of his head, discarded it again. "I never had an opinion about china, certainly never thought about the value of a wedding dress or veil. However, having been married this past year, I have begun to understand those things matter quite a bit to you ladies. Don't misunderstand me, it is certainly reasonable you would want what belongs to you."

Reaching into his pocket, he fished out his watch and placed it in Rebecca's hand. "One of my most treasured possessions is this pocket watch that belonged to my grandfather. Nothing flashy, purely serviceable, but it was his, and he gave it to me. Not valuable at all monetarily yet at the same time priceless."

Peter stood and resumed his pacing. Memories of a younger version of Peter flooded Rebecca's mind. She could picture him in almost the same spot, struggling as he prepared for his entrance to law school. Sensing he had stopped his pacing, Rebecca looked up as Peter took the chair beside her.

"Sorry, I was standing on the side of your bad ear. Let me begin again. Based on the custody papers, support payments were to be sent to a special account which reflects only one payment recorded years ago. There is no record of a request to change the method of payment. Which is why personally, I think it is all a ruse, perhaps a stall tactic and there may be little to nothing of your inheritance to be had."

Gathering her courage, Rebecca took a deep breath. "Frankly, my circumstances with no permanent job or place to live, dictates I try to find out. Now that my relationship with Sam is under such scrutiny, it seems providential my cousin invited me for a visit. If nothing else, my acceptance of the invitation will buy me some time."

Eyes wide, Peter leaned forward, saying, "Adam told me he'd encouraged you to visit with the Brooks' family. I know it is difficult for you to accept help from friends, much less from a relative you don't recall ever having met."

Rebecca glanced at her hands as she recalled the letter of instruction from Papa Horace she had received at the reading of his will.

...One of the reasons I encouraged you to write to your father was an effort to restore your relationship with him. You may remember although your father's English was excellent, his written communication was always conducted in German. After you were assured someone could read the letters to him, you never asked why he didn't write back. Writing seemed therapeutic for you, and we never had the heart to tell you that your correspondence was returned unopened. In retrospect, I am sorry for the deception and for not doing more to try and repair the relationship myself.

Because my time draws near, I have written to your mother's cousin Elizabeth, to ask for her help in this matter. She and her husband loved your mother and are well acquainted with your father...

Rebecca pushed her shoulders back. "It is more complicated than accepting help, I wondered why after all these years the invitation would be given. But since corresponding, I have learned she believed I was living back east for health reasons.

Now we all know the truth. She also offered to assist me in reconnecting with my father."

Pastor Nelson leaned forward. "Is there any reason you can give, why she shouldn't accept the invitation?"

Peter rubbed his chin. "No. The family's reputation is spotless. They are in good financial standing. If you would be willing to go next week, I can accompany you myself. We'd have to leave on Tuesday. Could you be ready by then?"

Rebecca found herself readily agreeing, "Yes, I would also like to continue with any legal proceedings necessary to get to the bottom of this. But as for your fee and the train ticket—I don't have the funds to pay you. And if things turn out as you said, I don't know if I ever could."

"All those hours you helped me prepare for law school ought to be worth something. How about we consider this my first installment in paying you back for your efforts?"

Taking her hand, Peter gave it a slight squeeze. "Honestly, our studying together helped me more than you will ever know. My father never understood why I struggled so with memorization. It was Horace's idea to get you to read aloud to me. It made all the difference. I am sorry I never told you both how much I appreciated the help."

Chapter 13

Dear Papa,
Papa Horace said since I cough so much when I am outside, it would be better to become an accountant instead of a traveling preacher. Aunt Eloise said I should be a seamstress...

Weary but feeling some relief at being home, Seth and Sam headed toward the barn to unload and take care of their horses. It had been a productive but long three days.

"Did you see who was in the buggy leaving as we drove up?" Sam asked.

"The only one around here I know who drives a buggy like that is the bank owner. Can't figure what he would be doing here. Maybe he wants to buy a saddle?"

Sam looked at Seth in surprise and chuckled. "He'd have to learn how to ride a horse first."

Laughing in agreement, Seth waived a greeting to his father, who was walking toward them at a faster pace than typical. "Looks like we are about to find out. Pa seems to have something on his mind."

Sam scanned the area around the house, his first concern for his girls. Everything looked to be in order, although now as he thought about it, perhaps it was more quiet than usual. "Everything okay, Adam? We haven't missed any payments at the bank, have we?"

"Good to see you back. You fellows made good time," Adam said, pounding his hand on Sam's back and bringing his son into a bear hug. "As far as payments go, I would tell you if we were in danger of being in arrears. Matt stopped by as more of a social call, I guess you would say," he said with a grin.

Both men stopped in their tracks. Sam eyed Adam suspiciously. "Social call? Since when do we get called on by bank owners?"

"Since today, I reckon." Adam wiped his face with his bandana. "We've had quite a few visits the last day or so. I guess you could say folks have been downright neighborly. See you, boys, after you get cleaned up." Winking, he continued, "Oh, a word to the wise, you might want to ask Cookie to set you something back for supper, seeing as how Emma has been cooking all morning."

Seth groaned, glaring at Sam. "I guess this means Rebecca is still madder than a hornet and our stomachs are going to pay for your comments."

Sam gazed at the big house upstairs window of the bedroom Rebecca typically used when she visited. "All I have been thinking about the last few hours is what I was going to say to her and wondering how I could make things right. I thought for sure she would be here. I've never known her not to spend her day off visiting Molly."

Glancing in the direction of Sam's gaze, Seth waived his hand in frustration. "Trust me; if she were here, we wouldn't be living in fear of having to eat Emma's cooking."

Adam grimaced at the smell coming from the kitchen, as he headed for the bedroom to check on Molly. "Emma you best inspect whatever you have in the oven. Girls your pa is home."

Emma gasped as she hurried to the oven.

"Burned them again," Sadie said as she gazed sadly at the pan of charred biscuits Emma withdrew.

"They don't look as bad as last night's," Grace added.

Waving the smoke away from the pan, Emma examined the biscuits. "Sometimes, I wonder why I even try. I am such a terrible cook." Glancing at the girls who were sitting uncharacteristically still at the kitchen table, she said, "You girls heard your Uncle Adam. Your father is home, don't you want to go see him?"

Grace nodded, as Sadie shook her head at her sister before answering. "We want to see him. But we don't want to talk to him yet."

Emma waved the smoke-filled kitchen with her apron. "I think I would like to postpone our talk myself. It might be best to give your pa a chance to get cleaned up and have a little something to eat first. Something in his stomach might put him in a better mood."

The twins stood up almost simultaneously in

silent communication.

"We best go now," Grace said diplomatically as Sadie wrinkled her nose in distaste at the burned biscuits.

Chapter 14

Dear Papa,
It is extremely cold this winter. Since Aunt Eloise is sick, Molly has come to live with us. She is teaching me to bake gingerbread cookies. We will decorate them for Christmas. I will save one for you. Please come...

Pastor Nelson and his family gathered together at one table in the front room in honor of Rebecca joining them for dinner. "Thank you for having me, Pastor and Mrs. Nelson. Everything was delicious."

Rebecca couldn't remember when she had eaten so much at one sitting. A simple, delicious meal of black-eyed peas, or cowpeas as some called them was served with small chunks of pork, along with sliced tomatoes, cornbread and a blackberry pie for dessert. The meal itself was economical and practical, but the combination of Mrs. Nelson's excellent cooking skills and the overall welcome she received gave her a feeling of happiness. "Let me do the cleaning up for you," Rebecca offered.

"Nonsense, the children will help. Boys, come finish your pie in the kitchen, so your father can speak with Miss Rebecca."

Rising to help her mother, Ruth leaned in closer to Rebecca, asking, "Which one is your good ear?"

Rebecca made a gesture motioning to the ear she could hear out of, and Ruth leaned in whispering, "I am so sorry, we didn't mean to embarrass you. Still, Mr. Anderson is nice and very handsome, don't you think? I think Helen's uncle is better looking though and she says he is as strong as an ox."

Martha Nelson called to her daughter from the kitchen. Rebecca felt her cheeks flame. She smiled and patted Ruth's hand without answering. What would make young girls act so? *I don't recall ever thinking about matchmaking at her age, not even at my age now.*

Pastor Nelson put on his reading glasses and moved his chair next to Rebecca. "Something you said at dinner about your recollection of Adam and Molly's wedding has me thinking. While it is true I believe how a person interacts with their parent is an indication of how they will get along with their spouse. It is not the only ingredient to a good relationship. Like all those recipes you and my wife are always chatting about, it is a lot of things blended together—some big, some small."

"You don't recall much about your mother since you were so young when she died. I can tell by the few things you can remember, that she loved you and you loved her back. Your father on the other hand, now that is a horse of a different color. What you remember is not good, and he's been absent for years."

Rebecca nodded as Pastor Nelson continued. "What I want you to understand is your relationship to God is the most important relationship you will ever have. Everything stems from how we view Him, how we feel about ourselves, others and how we treat them as well."

Opening his well-worn Bible, he asked, "Remember when the disciples asked Jesus to teach them to pray? He taught them to go to God as our Father in heaven. People can't seem to help compare their relationship with their earthly father to God; because that is what we know, see, hear and what we feel physically. I remember as a boy wondering why anyone would want another Father in heaven or anywhere else for that matter if he was anything like my old man."

Pastor Nelson paused and looked directly into Rebecca's eyes. "Rebecca, I want to ask you some personal questions about how you see God. Not what you have been taught but how you view Him. To you, who is Jesus?"

"He is God's son, who is fully God and fully man. He has been and always was and came to earth to live a perfect life and die on the cross for our sins. He died, was resurrected, and one day He is coming again."

Pastor Nelson with a smile acknowledged, "How do you know?

"The Bible, the word of God, tells us," Rebecca

answered again.

"Do you believe it?

"Yes, I believe it."

"Do you believe He hears your prayers?"

Puzzled, she stammered, "Well…yes. I know God hears them. Though, I don't know that He always answers them."

Pausing, Pastor Nelson tapped his glasses lightly on his Bible. "God is not flawed like our earthly fathers. He has a personal interest in your life and knows the number of hairs you have on your head. Frankly, that is a lot of hair." Laughing at his joke, he touched his slightly receding hairline. "God doesn't have near the same amount to keep up with on me."

Rebecca found herself smiling at the pastor's remark as he continued.

"I fail as a Father because I am a mortal man. Your earthly father failed you. God supplied other men like Horace and your papas here in town to fill in some of the gaps. As mortals we make poor decisions, we sin, we are flawed. God is not. He knows everything about you, loves you and wants the best for you. He understands your pain and wants to offer you comfort. Do you understand what I am saying?"

"Yes, I think so. You don't want my relationship with God, to be like the one I have with my Father."

"The main thing I am concerned about—especially after hearing how you found the unopened letters to your father—is that you might think God views your prayers in the same way."

Rebecca winced. "Papa Horace always said, 'God knows our thoughts, so he knows what we think even if we never speak it.'"

"I would agree. But I will also add, God takes pleasure in hearing from you. He wants to comfort, guide, and protect you. There are no unopened letters to God, Rebecca. Take your time to seek Him. He will give you an answer."

Rebecca's lips quivered. "Thank you, Pastor, that is a salve which goes straight to the heart."

"Let's pray about it together, shall we?"

Chapter 15

Dear Papa,
Aunt Eloise went to heaven today. I will miss her...

Sam raked his hand through his hair as he stared at his daughters. "Girls, hopefully, I didn't hear you right. Tell me again you did what?"

"What did you hear exactly?" Sadie asked cocking her head at her father with concern.

Sam, groaned. Just when he was thinking things couldn't get any worse as far as his relationship with Rebecca was concerned, the girls pulled something like this. "Are you telling me you asked your friends to help Rebecca find a husband by writing an ad for the paper? That can't be true. You don't even know all of your letters yet."

Grace looked up in shock. "We know all our letters. We just don't always put them in their proper place."

Sadie crossed her arms over her chest

incredulously, agreeing with her sister. "That is why we asked Mary Ellen to help."

"Mary Ellen?" Sam furrowed his brow. "Remind me, which one is Mary Ellen?"

"The smart one," Grace said.

"Kate is the rich one, Sadie added

"There she goes again." Grace said rolling her eyes. "Kate is Sadie's best friend. That's why she wants Rebecca to marry *her pa*."

"Who is Kate's pa?"

"He owns the bank," Sadie said smiling.

Sam moaned and stared at Emma who wore a strange look on her face. "Was her father leaving as we were riding up?"

Wide-eyed, Emma nodded.

Thinking back to Adam's remark about the banker's visit being a social one, Sam threw his hands in the air in frustration. "Everyone in this house seems to be scheming against me. What in tarnation, girls? Why do you think Rebecca needs help finding a husband? I thought you both loved her and wanted me to marry her?"

Both girls' mouths dropped open, looking at each other in perfect mirror image. Except for a small, faded scar above Grace's lip placed there by Sadie a few years back, they were near to impossible to tell apart until they began to talk. "Pa," they said in unison.

"You said you didn't want her," Grace frowned, crossing her arms across her chest.

"You said she was a castoff," Sadie growled.

"Now hold on a minute, I didn't do any such thing."

Grace gasped. "Pa, that is a fib."

"Girls, I will not have you correcting me. I am your father." Frustrated, Sam rubbed his temples as he turned to Emma. "Help me out here, what is going on?"

Emma answered hesitantly. "It was hardly a quiet conversation. The girls and everyone, me included, heard the argument—I mean conversation—you had with Rebecca. We all understood you to be breaking things off."

Sam shook his head in frustration. "I never said any such thing."

Emma cocked her head and raised her eyebrows in answer.

Thinking back, Sam remembered being annoyed because he hadn't felt at peace about his finances and had not set a date for the wedding. Some of the hired hands had been teasing him about Rebecca's admirers. Adam also offered an opinion.

"Sam, when was the last time you were in town? It's not the same place it was six months ago. I'm telling you a young single girl living on her own is asking for trouble. I never liked the fact Rebecca was staying at the boarding house, though at the time it seemed safe enough. But not now. Soon she won't have that measly little room, then what?"

The problem was he didn't know what Rebecca was going to do. When she mentioned she wasn't going to be able to afford to stay at the boarding house, he assumed she might be exaggerating the circumstances and needed to budget better. And if she was so short on money, what was she doing buying the girls dresses?

"Now hold on there, wait a minute. I was mad and overreacted." Taking a breath, he kneeled to get eye level with his daughters. "Girls, I appreciate what Rebecca does, but it's my job to take care of you. Whatever you girls need, I will provide. Rebecca needs to take care of herself."

"See, you did say it," Sadie said crossly.

"Say what? Girls this isn't making any sense."

Emma walked over to the twins. "Let me talk to your pa for a few minutes. You two go visit with Molly. I bet she would enjoy your company."

Huffing, Sadie stomped off, but Grace held back, hesitating for a moment before following her sister from the room.

Her cheeks hot from frustration, Emma faced Sam. "I think I am beginning to understand a little bit better why you reacted the way you did. You forget one thing though. I was there when she showed you the fabric."

Sam massaged his temples. "Whenever you women start talking about fabric, how much is needed and patterns and all, it makes my head ache. I will admit I was probably wool-gathering when she showed it to me."

"She came by the material because of some work she's been doing for Lois. Rebecca does trading all the time. For instance, she is teaching the blacksmith's daughter how to sew, which is how she got her horse re-shod."

Upon reflection, Rebecca had been stating facts as far as her room and board. Something he should have been concerned about. "Alright, I have made a lot of assumptions. Obviously, I made a mistake about the dresses. If I'd an objection, I should have said something earlier. But I did not call her a castoff."

Emma's eyebrows drew together, reminding Sam of Sadie which made him chuckle. "Okay, I know that expression. Rebecca is not here which is unusual for a Saturday. Even if she was mad at me, I can't imagine her giving up an opportunity to spend time with you and Molly. The girls are so upset, they are trying to find Rebecca a husband. Please enlighten me."

Emma's mouth dropped. "I believe the exact quote was, she was wearing other people's castoffs, and her boots have patches on their patches. But we all thought you wanted her to stay out of your life."

Running his hands through his hair, Sam groaned, "That is not what I meant. I don't want her doing without because she is worried about my girls. I can take care of them myself."

Emma frowned and placed her hands on her hips. "Rebecca loves your girls and takes pleasure in doing for them. You should have seen her planning the design of the dresses, right down to fretting which buttons to use. She had us all at the table trying to figure out how to get the most out of the material. I recollect she asked you to stay. You gave her some excuse about being behind on your saddle orders and not being able to spare the time."

Sam ran his hand through his hair again, which was now standing on end. "I've made a mess of things. Our relationship has been strained since I felt like she was pressuring me to marry right away. I do not want to set a date until I have my finances in order and not until I am sure our relationship is ready for the next step."

"Sam," Emma exclaimed, "Then you did mean to break things off?"

"No, I was angry. You've seen yourself how thin Rebecca is getting. Truthfully, I was mad at myself for not noticing before now."

"Rebecca doesn't deserve to be treated that way. I saw her crying her eyes out. It's not like Rebecca to lose control. I have never seen her so hurt."

"You are right. She sure is not one to cry. I hate it I was the one to cause her tears. I was wrong and will apologize and make her understand what I meant."

Huffing Emma responded, "Good luck with that. Because it sounded to everyone, including your girls, you were ending things. Let's not forget the fact you said she looked like a fence post."

Sam's mouth dropped open. "That is not what I said."

Chapter 16

Dear Papa,
Papa Horace said Aunt Eloise is spending time with Jesus. Do you think when she is done she will speak with Mama too?

A few minutes before closing, Lois surprised Rebecca with the dress she refashioned from Molly's old one. "I want you to have another dress to wear when you go to visit your mother's family. Why don't you scoot on in the back and try it on? I can't wait to see how it fits."

The dress was a blue wildflower calico with full sleeves gathered to a cuff. Rebecca admired her reflection in the full-length mirror as she examined the three-paneled skirt with pockets and a slightly scooped neckline with front button closure.

"The dress is beautiful Lois, and I love the pockets. I don't think I have ever worn something so pretty. With this dress and the two blouses you made me, I won't have to go to meet my mother's relatives dressed like a ragamuffin."

Lois tilted her head to the left and right, finally doing a circle around Rebecca, she declared, "Yes, it is quite the success. Don't forget to tell all your new friends and family about your dressmaker," she said with a grin. "Besides, you have worked so hard to help me, you deserve this and more. It's a shame you don't have another pair of boots though. Those have definitely seen better days."

Spinning around to examine her dress in the mirror again, Rebecca replied, "With a dress this pretty, who cares what my shoes look like?"

Although proficient, Rebecca's skills were nothing compared to Lois's as she could fairly fly through the work using her Singer sewing machine. "Since you aren't going to be leaving until Tuesday, I should have your other dress finished as well."

Rebecca squealed, "Oh, I never believed you would have time. Are you sure? I wouldn't want to keep you from your other work."

"Of course, I am sure. Besides, if it weren't for your ideas, your friend, and her daughter, I would be closing up shop for good about right now."

"I am proud my dress design and some of the dolls were a success. Thank goodness the supply train finally came through. The fabric selection you have is the prettiest so far. I can't wait to see what my plaid dress will look like."

Lois replied stoically. "Much like the one you are wearing, but plaid."

Rebecca gasped in surprise and then caught the twinkle in Lois's eyes. Hearing the bell, signaling a customer, Rebecca joked, "I'll see who it is. You better get to work on my dress."

Rebecca turned from closing the dressing room door and came to a halt and stared at Sam. *What was he doing here?* Blinking, she looked again. It was Sam alright; she would recognize those blue eyes anywhere. Rebecca couldn't help but think how handsome he was. His skin had a golden tone from exposure to the sun, his hair was trimmed, and he was freshly shaved. Turning to head back to the dressing room, she said, "Lois is in the back, I will get her for you."

"Rebecca, wait, I am not here to see Lois. I have been all over town searching for you."

Stopping for a moment, she turned slightly as Sam made up the distance between them. "Nobody would give me a straight answer. Finally, Mrs. Potts told me you were here. You look real pretty by the way."

Flushing as she remembered their last conversation and his reference to her appearance, she felt her anger resurface. "What is it you want, Sam?"

"I want to talk with you, to apologize."

"Alright, apology accepted. Now if you will excuse me." Rebecca turned and reentered the dressing room, nearly knocking Lois over.

Lois rubbed her ear. "Goodness Rebecca. Give me a little warning next time."

Calling through the door, Sam pleaded, "Rebecca, come on now, honey. I know you are mad and you have every right to be. Please hear me out."

Rebecca placed her back against the closed

door. "I don't think there is anything left to say. You were very clear."

"I have plenty to say. Becca, I want to do this right. Please, open the door."

Lois leaned forward, offering her a hug and a pat on her shoulder. "Things can't get any worse between you two. Might as well hear the man out."

With a tilt to her chin, Rebecca slid the latch and opened the door. Her hands clenched into fists as she glared at Sam.

Removing his hat and with a quick smile, he rushed to speak, "I was hoping maybe we could go somewhere and talk. Mrs. Potts made us some supper. How about we go on the picnic I've been promising you?"

Seeing no benefit to postponing and not wanting Lois to hear their conversation, Rebecca agreed.

Sam hurried to open the door, allowing Rebecca to pass through first. As she turned to leave she saw Lois smile at Sam and mouth the words, "Good luck."

Sam glanced around the town as he helped Rebecca into the wagon. "I can see what you mean about how things have changed in town, what with the high prices and all. You sure wouldn't know this is a dry county by the looks of some of those fellows."

Rebecca laughed. "You haven't seen anything yet."

Nothing else was said as he headed for a favorite location for the locals to picnic. Sam pulled onto a flat area near the river, jumped down and reached to help Rebecca from the wagon. "It took me a while, but after I assured Mrs. Potts I was trying to make things right, she grudgingly made us a picnic basket."

From the look of the hamper, Rebecca imagined it set him back a pretty penny. *I should be ashamed of myself, but the thought that Mrs. Potts gave him a bad time, is satisfying.*

Taking the basket, Sam followed Rebecca closer to the river where she sat on a rock perched onto another boulder creating a makeshift table.

"I see you have found us the perfect spot," Sam said.

Studying the flow of the river, she answered without looking at him. "I came here a lot before things started to get so rough in town. It's not safe to come by myself anymore."

"Rebecca, I want you to know how sorry I am about everything. I never intended to hurt you."

Lifting her chin defiantly, she said, "What exactly was your intention?"

Taking her hand in his, he said, "My aim was to court and marry you. I've made some poor decisions based on my feelings of inadequacy. I've been too focused on my own thoughts and never stopped to listen to yours. I want you to know how sorry I am."

Rebecca stared back at him, her eyes flashing in anger, "So you have said."

"You don't believe me?"

Rebecca removed her hand from Sam's and turned toward the river. "What is this all about? If all this is simply for you to apologize, it is not necessary. Although I wish you would have been more forthcoming earlier in our relationship if you meant to break things off."

Exhaling sharply, Sam retook Rebecca's hand. "It was not my intention to break things off. I don't want you to worry about my girls, especially since you have been struggling to make ends meet." Clearing his throat, he continued, "About the comments on your appearance. It was a poor choice of words, and it came out all wrong. I am sorry. Surely, you realize how beautiful you are? The reason you always have men swarming around you is not just because you are so sweet."

Pulling her hand away again, Rebecca turned and walked closer to the river. Bending she picked up a flat stone and ran her thumb across it, feeling the smoothness.

Sam's body cast a shadow as Rebecca studied the stone. "If it will make you feel better, you can throw it at me." Raising his eyebrows in question and with a grin, he added, "I will even stand still for you to do it."

Smiling a little at his playful manner, Rebecca looked away, not wanting to meet his gaze. "Nothing I do makes you happy, Sam. So again, I am asking why you are here?"

She turned around slightly, regarding him. Sam rubbed his hand through his hair, then spoke softly. "Rebecca, you make me very happy. But I let my pride get in the way and stall things unnecessarily. On the one hand, I was worried about finances, and on the other, I thought it would be a matter of time before you said yes to one of those fellows in town. Figured you would be better off too."

Crossing her arms and tapping her foot, Rebecca asked. "Don't you mean to say, you thought *you* would be better off without me?"

Sam felt his jaw drop. *How can I make her understand she means everything to me?* "I can see I have made you feel unwanted. I want to fix this. Becca, look at me," Sam pleaded.

Arms still crossed, she nodded, "Alright, I'm looking."

Sam took a deep breath. "I don't want you having to worry about money. I want to provide for us. You are beautiful, smart, loving, and way too good for someone like me. I do love you and want you to be my wife. If I believed you would agree I would take you to the preacher right now, say my vows and mean them with everything in me."

Staring at the smooth stone still in her hand, she whispered, "I wish I could believe you, but I don't."

Taking her chin and lifting her face to his, he spoke softly. "What can I do to make you believe me?"

Rebecca blinked rapidly to keep her tears from falling. "I don't know that you can."

"Honey, please listen. I will make you the happiest woman in Texas. Part of the problem is I have been allowing the difficulties in my first marriage to affect our relationship. I want to correct that. Let's start over. I'll court you, the way I should have done in the first place. What can I do to prove to you how much I love you?"

Rebecca wiped the tears away with both hands. "Maybe, you can write to me while I am gone. We can begin there."

"Write you? What do you mean, where are you going?"

"I've decided to visit my mother's family, the cousin I told you about. They have offered to help me when I go to meet my father or at least meet with his attorney."

"Now hold on a minute. When did you make that decision? I thought you were going to wait until we got married before you went to meet with anybody."

"I can't afford the boarding house any longer and don't want to impose on friends to take me in and feed me. So, I took the only option with merit. I honestly didn't think you cared what I did."

"Not care?" Retaking her hand, he pulled her into an embrace, holding her close. "Of course, I care. Don't go. Molly and Adam would be happy for you to stay with them. Let me try and make this up to you. Then we can get married, and I can take you to meet your father, in the spring."

"I would have given anything for you to say this to me last month. Maybe even last week. But you didn't. I've chosen to go visit my cousins." Rebecca pulled back and searched his expression. "I would love to believe you. If you are serious about this, write to me, while I am gone."

Sam took off his hat and wiped his hands through his hair. "There is something I should have shared with you before now." His face flushed. He took in a deep breath, exhaling slowly. "When I was a boy, I had a hard time sitting still in school. The teacher and my pa didn't agree on how I should be disciplined. So, he felt I would be better off with him on the farm. Pa taught me leather work and basic things like ciphering, but I've had very little book learning."

Rebecca bit her lip as she considered. She had never noticed anything that would suggest Sam's education was lacking. He was a talented saddle maker and could calculate in his head almost as quickly as she could.

"This must be hard for you to imagine, being as smart as you are," he said. "I'm not exaggerating when I say my reading and writing skills are not much better than the girls'. Even so, if that is what it takes for you to know I'm serious, you can bet your bottom dollar, I will give it a try. But I don't want to disappoint you."

Rebecca reached for Sam's hand and smiled. "That is an excellent start, Sam Brady."

Drawing her back into his arms and holding her close, he whispered, "You can count on it then. I do love you, Rebecca."

Chapter 17

Dear Papa,
Papa Horace is very sad. He enjoys when I read aloud his law books. I don't like it very much, but I pretend that I do. Do you think Jesus is upset about that?

Taking her seat next to the window, Rebecca waived to Sam as the train slowly chugged forward, concealing her view with steam. He handed her a note as she was boarding. "I drew you a picture this time. But I will keep my promise. Please write to me when you can."

Looking at it now, it was a perfect sketch of Sadie and Grace sitting on the back of her horse. "Oh, it's beautiful," she said softly.

Noticing Rebecca's gaze, Peter leaned forward and remarked, "Fine picture, glad to see you two are working things out. If you like, we can send a wire to let Sam know we arrived."

Surprised by his thoughtfulness, Rebecca

smiled. "Thank you, Peter. I do appreciate what you are doing for me."

"Happy to do it. There are a few things I hoped we could work on while we are on our way. No sense letting an opportunity get away from me." Peter smiled apologetically. "I never had your eye for bookkeeping, so I was hoping you would look something over to see if you can determine where the discrepancy is."

Smiling in agreement, Rebecca took the ledger he held out and flipped through the first two years of records, quickly comparing expenses and profits. "The first thing I notice is it is very neat, tidy, concise. Perhaps a little too tidy."

Rebecca continued to examine the pages then paused and tapped her index finger against her mouth.

Peter chuckled. "I recognize that gesture as one my father used whenever he solved a problem. "You've already got this figured out, don't you?"

"Is this a friend of yours?"

"No, definitely not a friend."

Rebecca leaned closer and extended the ledger so that Peter could get a better view. "Notice the first year and how the columns line up; everything is rounded to the next dollar. This makes me wonder if this is a record of estimates, not actuals. Now note the price per head, for cattle. I don't know anything about this rancher, but the sales appear to be consistently one full dollar less than the going rate each year. Does that make sense?"

Shaking his head and with a chuckle, he answered. "I confess the average price for cattle is not something I am familiar enough with to quote. But I have a feeling you are about to enlighten me. Please proceed."

Tapping her pencil against her cheek, she explained. "Circumstances may necessitate a rancher getting less than the going rate, but each year, for exactly one dollar? If this is a reputable rancher, with good stock, I would say someone is lining his pockets. It is fairly easy to check the cattle records of the shipping facility he used."

Shaking his head, Peter said, "You amaze me with your head for numbers. I paid an accountant to examine these records. He sure didn't mention the going rate for cattle."

Feeling the camaraderie, they had when they were younger, Rebecca exclaimed, "Pricing was a daily part of my schooling at home with Papa Horace. He didn't always use traditional books, but he found plenty to help me learn and keep me busy. I always found it interesting. He would have me work his figures on profitability, in livestock, and all sorts of things. Since I have been working at the diner, most of the men in town discuss the cost of goods and services right down to the value of a good cowhand."

Noting Peter was watching her intently, she continued. "It might seem silly to you, but you would be surprised by the information that can be learned in that kind of setting."

"No, not silly at all. Leave it to you to always be learning something new. I've often wondered why you went to work there. I assumed you enjoyed meeting new people and working with Mrs. Potts.

But it was more than that, wasn't it?"

Rebecca hesitated. Although the work at the law office was fulfilling, the environment was strained after Peter had taken over the business. "It was a lot of things. Although, I didn't think I would be working at the diner so long."

Peter stiffened his posture, yet his expression was kind. "Rebecca, when things got hard for you in town, why didn't you let me know?"

"You have a business to run, a new wife; I didn't want to be a burden to you."

"A burden? In this one instance alone, you could have saved me both time and money. Besides, you are like family to me. Would you consider coming back to work for me again? We can offer you a place to stay. I am sure Sally would enjoy having another woman to talk to."

Rebecca didn't know how to answer. Knowing Peter was in earnest didn't take away the fact she understood his wife would be less than pleased.

Peter frowned. "Sally said something to you, didn't she?"

Rebecca's mouth dropped involuntarily. "I never mentioned anything to anyone."

Shaking his head and staring at the ceiling, he said, "No one had to say anything. I love my wife. However, she can be arrogant, and self-serving. So out with it, young lady. You will not be the first of my friends she offended."

"It is not important. I don't believe I have seen your wife since you were married, except from a distance. So please don't worry about it."

Peter muttered something under his breath.

"We've known each other for years. Out with it. Don't try and minimize whatever it was. At this point, I don't know if I can even be surprised anymore."

Rebecca lowered her eyes and folded her hands in her lap. "She asked me not to attend the engagement party your father hosted. She said she would make some excuse as to why I wasn't there."

Seemingly dumbstruck, Peter stammered, "Honestly, I don't remember you not being present. I was so overwhelmed by the whole thing. I can't apologize enough."

"I admit to feeling some relief knowing you weren't of the same opinion. Let's not mention it again."

"Sally and her father will most likely meet us at the station. Let me take advantage of this opportunity to say this. My wife's opinions are often contrary to mine and have caused a great deal of discord in our marriage. Be assured of this, you will be treated with the utmost respect from this point on, and I won't have to say one word to make it come about." Peter leaned back in his chair and erupted in laughter, slapping his knee in merriment.

Several people turned their head curiously, infected by his mirth and smiled. Still perplexed at his continued more subdued laughter, Rebecca asked, "what in the world is so funny?"

"Once my wife sees who is meeting you at the station and understands you are related to and will be staying with one of the most influential families in this part of Texas, she will be green with envy. I can't wait to see the look on her face," Peter declared as he again roared with laughter.

Chapter 18

Dear Papa,
Papa Horace and I spend most of our time at his friend's law office. He thinks I will make an exceptional law clerk. I much prefer working with numbers…

Peter Marks entered the prestigious law office of Jonas Weber's brother, Jacob, who left the comfort of his beautiful leather chair and extended his hand in greeting. "Right on time, I see. Peter, you are Johnny-on-the-spot. What can I do for you?"

Peter glanced at documents outlining the petition on the attorney's desk. "I am here at your request, Jacob, to discuss Rebecca Mueller."

"Pardon my confusion. My legal assistant assured me he answered your questions in a previous meeting. We are both successful, busy men. Since time is money as they say, what is this about?"

Peter took a seat at the edge of the desk. "Your reputation as a lawyer is excellent. Therefore, I find it hard to believe you would intentionally be negligent of the estate belonging to a client of yours." Seeing the fury cross Jacob's face at the accusation, Peter continued, "Let me be clear, it is my belief you have been deceived. What I would like to know is whether you would like for me to enlighten you now or in court?"

Jacob Weber's face flushed red with anger, yet he answered in a controlled voice. "You intrigue me, what causes you to question the integrity of this law firm?"

"For clarity let me recap. You believe Charles Mueller has been providing for his daughter Rebecca, financially at first to her guardian, later for a boarding school, and currently a finishing school for young ladies?"

Glancing at his notes, Jacob Weber said, "Yes an allotment is sent each year to the school along with additional money necessary for painting, music lessons, boarding, and clothing. There has also been a considerable amount allotted for her to have the required medical attention due to her unfortunate health issues. You have seen the figures."

Peter picked up the journal. "Rebecca Mueller, until recently, never left Carrie Town. She was schooled at home. In fact, the only boarding she's been involved in was at a boarding house where she lived on her own the last few years, barely making ends meet. The one thing we can agree on is, substantial funds have been withdrawn or rather they were embezzled from her trust fund."

Narrowing his eyes, Jacob Weber pointed at the satchel plump with documentation laying partially open on the chair Peter vacated. "Exactly what do you have that proves your claim, sir?"

"Birth, baptism records, affidavits of witnesses, medical records. Additionally, perhaps the most compelling is years of correspondence Rebecca sent to her father which was returned unopened."

Jacob Weber's eyebrows knitted together. "Charles Mueller is a hard man, it is true. However, I would never believe this of him. There must be some mistake. I cannot believe he would deny his daughter in this way."

Peter withdrew a stack of letters from his satchel addressed to Charles Mueller. "Look closely Jacob, a small sampling of years of letters to a father who refused to bother to read them."

Jacob rubbed his chin as he considered Peter's statement. "When I took over Charles's legal affairs initially, he always became agitated discussing any details regarding Becky. Naturally, I assumed it was from the stress of her illness. The last ten years or so he sent his wife or accountant for any business needs. Frankly, my assistant handles all of that." Jacob flipped through the records from the file on his desk. "We have letters on file from the school giving details on her academic progress and how she was progressing socially. There is certainly no evidence any of these details were falsified."

"Perhaps, you need more time to review this new information, to decide how best to proceed. I am leaving you with a copy of the doctor's report, along with the affidavits of the witnesses. Keep the returned letters. Unfortunately, there are years of additional examples where those came from. We will be in town for the next few days. Afterward, Rebecca will be visiting the Brooks' family ranch. She would like to become reacquainted with her father, so I will leave it to you to set a time to meet. However, if you have not done so within the month, I will see you in court."

Somberly, Jacob extended his hand to Peter. "Rest assured the matter will be investigated fully."

Putting on his hat to leave, Peter added, "If this were me and the shoe was on the other foot, I would produce the Rebecca Mueller who has been the recipient of a large sum of money. I also would be investigating your accountant."

"He is not my accountant, Mr. Marks. The accountant Mr. Mueller uses is his own, a Mr. James Taylor. I've never had reason to question him before. He turns his receipts in timely, never anything out of line. Nevertheless, I see your point. I will proceed most carefully."

The elimination of the use of his first name was not lost to Peter. *So be it.* "It seems we will have to go about this the hard way."

Chapter 19

Dear Papa,
Today is March 30, 1885, my 15th birthday. Papa Horace said I was born on the day that Congress readmitted Texas into the Union. He is not feeling well. I am worried about him. It is a comfort Papa Horace's other nephew arrived to help.

Sam struggled with the process of the final steps of the saddle he'd been working on. Everything was assembled except for the wrapping of the horn. He had already wrapped it several times, fighting to get the stretch out, when he heard his girls squealing. From the moment they were born, six years ago, he had been amazed at the sounds that could come from such tiny little bodies. Stopping his work for a quick moment, he focused again on the noise and smiled as he realized they were pleased about something.

"Pa, Pa, we got a letter."

"I was hoping that was what all the noise was about. Come on in here and read it to me. I am not at a place where I can stop."

"Is it okay if we open it, Pa?" Grace asked.

"He is teasing us, Gracie. He knows we don't read that good," Sadie said with a snort.

Grace corrected, "Well. He knows we don't read well."

Sadie studied her sister for a moment then put her hand on her hips. "That is what I said."

Laughing softly at their antics but sensing a battle, Sam corrected his daughters. "Girls enough is enough. Grace would you go see if Emma can come read it to us? If she can't, we will have to wait until I can turn loose of this saddle."

Sam watched as Grace happily complied. Sadie followed, united over a common goal. His gut clenched as he wondered again if Rebecca would want to come back after spending all these weeks hobnobbing with folks who spent more money in a week than he made all year. *No one would blame her if she doesn't after I treated her like I did.*

Silently he prayed, *Lord, please let me be able to make it up to her. Allow me to be the husband and father you want me to be. Help me, so my desires are yours. Please, Lord.*

Turning back to his work, he attacked the leather with a vengeance.

Sam ran his hand along the saddle, smiling as he admired the fruits of his labor. He couldn't help but be proud of how it was turning out. A couple more orders should allow him to be able to pay his share of the taxes. Maybe then he could relax a little.

Deep in thought, he was jolted back to reality as he heard the girls' voices again. What was it about girls and their squeals, he wondered, as Emma came into view being dragged into the barn by the twins. He smiled again, thinking how much they looked like his niece. "I see the girls wouldn't take no for an answer."

"No, they certainly didn't." Emma patted the girls' backs. "However, I was happy to come. I will be glad to read your letter."

"Please, go ahead with the girls' part. We can read mine later," he said as he felt his cheeks redden.

Emma set on the bench beside the girls. Clearing her throat, she read.

Dear Grace and Sadie,

I hope this letter finds you well and that you are both being good.

Emma paused, raising her eyebrows in question.

"It would be a lot easier to be good if Sadie wasn't always trying to tell me what to do," Grace said.

Sadie gasped. "I don't tell you what to do, but what *not* to do."

Clearing his throat, Sam interrupted. "Girls, do you want to hear your letter or not?"

Taking his meaning, they sat as still as possible, waiting for Emma to continue.

I miss you both so much. I am comforted by the beautiful picture your Pa drew for me. I look at his sketches and the beautiful drawing you sent in your last letter every day.

This past week I have stayed at the ranch. They

have a lot of beautiful horses. I find I can ride in the morning during the cool portion of the day without a single cough. They also have pigs, chickens, sheep, and goats. The baby goats are so funny and seem to always run in circles or stand on each other's backs.

My cousins employ a cook here. She makes the most wonderful fried chicken. She promises me she will be able to teach me to make it. She is continuously tempting me with something fresh from the oven. Everyone is always trying to get me to eat something no matter where I go. Soon I shall grow to be quite fat.

I miss you all.
Much love,
Rebecca.

"Pa, can we get a baby goat?" Grace asked.

"Can we get two? That way we can see them stand on each other's back. One could be for me and the other for Grace," Sadie asked hopefully.

Chuckling, Sam explained, "Rebecca's cousin's family live in hill country. Since the land there is different the sheep and goats keep the weeds controlled, which allows the grass to grow for the cattle."

Molly had helped Sam read Rebecca's previous letters, which described the beautiful scenery at the Brooks' ranch with its green hills and crystal-clear water, a striking contrast to the area around Carrie Town which was mostly flat. She described the terrain as breathtaking yet challenging to manage.

Chuckling to himself, Sam thought, leave it to Rebecca to take the time to learn the ins and outs of ranching in hill country.

"I don't know what Uncle Adam would think about bringing goats here. We will have to do some studying on that."

Grace nodded, but Sadie pressed the issue. "I think a goat sounds much more interesting, don't you Pa? Maybe Uncle Adam should sell all the cattle and get goats, instead?"

Emma laughed. "Come on, you two. Help me set the table. Let's allow your Pa to finish his work, so maybe he can join us."

Sadie narrowed her eyebrows. "Did you or Uncle Adam make supper?"

"Uncle Adam has been working outside all day, so I made it. I am trying out a new recipe. I think you will like it."

Watching her father as he turned back to his saddle making, Sadie replied, "I believe Pa has too much work left to do to join us for supper."

Sadie ran to her father with extended arms. "I love you, Pa. Whispering into his ear, she added, "Ask Cookie to save us something to eat, please."

Chapter 20

Dear Papa
I fear I will never be the elegant lady Aunt Eloise wanted me to be. It is so much more gratifying to work with numbers and to read about the law than to try and make little flowers with my stitching. I am afraid I was a great disappointment to her...

After weeks of attempts, Jacob Weber finally managed to meet with Charles Mueller, a man who was continuously at work on his 75,000-acre ranch. At first glance, the wealth he now amassed could not be noted in his simple attire of denim work pants and vest, except upon closer inspection of his boots. He'd begun wearing the more practical pointy-toe boot, knee-high design pulled on by mule-ear straps years ago, but they now were made of superior leather, and sported patterns in colorful threads.

"I don't believe it." This is some hoax of

Elizabeth Brooks. She only wants to get control of Becky's inheritance. I would never have believed she would stoop so low. Leah would be heartbroken."

"Charles, the information Mr. Marks presented is persuasive, which is why I would like for us to go over the evidence. The facts are so compelling, if we were to go to court today, a judge could be persuaded in their favor."

"Nonsense, what could she know about my daughter? It is reprehensible of you to insist I come to your office for this nonsense. You are wasting my time."

"This meeting would not be necessary if I were not at least convinced of the validity of the facts. Pausing, Jacob watched for his reaction. "Charles, when was the last time you saw Becky in person?"

Silenced filled the room as pain crossed the large man's face. It was still a handsome face, although weathered by the many hours in the sun. His eyes, a light blue speckled with green and encircled by a darker blue, closed as he reflected on the question. "I have not been permitted to see her since she was five years old."

"After reviewing the custody papers your former lawyer drew up, the intention was not that you should never see her, rather she would never be alone in the presence of your wife."

"Do not speak of things you know nothing about," Charles snarled."

"There is no doubt this is going to be painful. Whatever the custody agreements were at the time, they are no longer valid at this point as Rebecca turned eighteen months ago."

"I am aware of how old my daughter is." Charles clenched his jaw.

"We can continue in this manner, nipping at each other's heels and getting nowhere, or we can get down to facts. I have reviewed the documents presented, including a detailed report from a private investigator. Unless you can provide me with information proving differently, it seems likely, until recently, your daughter never left Carrie Town. She has been living on her own in extremely reduced circumstances for the last two years."

Charles' hands clenched beside him, curling and uncurling in fists. "That is a lie."

Saying nothing further, Jacob Weber reached for the stack of unopened correspondence written by Rebecca. He laid them out on his desk. "Take a look at these letters in a child's handwriting. They are all addressed to you and marked return to sender by the post office."

Watching carefully for any sign of recognition or any emotion, he waited for a response. Charles glanced at the envelopes quickly as though he didn't see the importance. "What is this nonsense?"

Jacob picked up one of the envelopes which had been cast aside. "I would like for you to examine these letters, to see if you recognize the handwriting. Do you ever recall receiving a letter like this from your daughter?"

Head down, Charles thumbed through the unopened letters now yellowed with age. "Yes, I received a letter much like this one after Eloise died. Which is how I recognized Becky would need someone to fill in where Horace could not."

"What we need at this point is to produce your daughter in court. There would be no legal reason for you not to visit. Or, with your permission, we could send a reputable investigator to prove her whereabouts. In the meantime, I personally would like to interview your accountant."

"You have my permission. Now, if that is all, I have work to do." Charles scowled, put on his hat and left the office."

Stunned at his reaction, Jacob called for his assistant. As he returned to his desk, he noticed the letters were missing. Perhaps, the man was not so heartless after all?

Chapter 21

Dear Papa,
This winter seems to be even more severe than last year. How are you fairing? I fear Papa Horace is not going to make it to Christmas. I will miss him so, and yet I can't help wondering where I will live when he passes...

Rebecca enjoyed her visit with her cousins, especially the time spent with Elizabeth and her youngest daughter Sara Jane, at their family's ranch. They spent countless hours riding horseback, exploring the beautiful paths which included sprawling pastures, dense trails of wildflowers and the apple orchard. Elizabeth had taken great pride in explaining the family's background.

"Although your mother's love turned more to horses, she agreed with your father's vision to raise cattle. The original investment for this property and your parent's ranch was almost totally funded by a gift from your great-grandfather. He meant it as a legacy to pass from generation to generation."

The leisure time Rebecca was allotted was unlike anything she could remember in the past years. The cooler temperature, as well as the abundance of good food, rest, and exercise, improved her health, and her coughing had diminished.

Much to her delight, Sara Jane enlisted her help in designing new dresses for the upcoming parties in town. They worked together to repurpose some old gowns they found stored in the attic. The new creations were off-the-shoulder designs with bow accented sleeves and fitted bodices that dipped to a figure-flattering V at the waist. Sara Jane selected a champagne colored, striped silk brocade. Rebecca's was blue silk.

Upon seeing the completed products, Elizabeth was elated. "You girls couldn't look any prettier. You are both so alike in appearance. It was the same for your mother and me. We were often mistaken for sisters." Although it was true, the physical characteristics of honey-colored hair and blue eyes were similar. It was the actual feeling of belonging to a family that was pleasing to Rebecca. But as much as Rebecca looked forward to attending parties and meeting new friends, she found herself reluctant to leave the ranch.

"Are you excited about going back into town, Rebecca?" Elizabeth asked.

Sara Jane glanced at Rebecca, not waiting for an answer. "What a silly question, Mama. Of course, she is. I can't wait to show her the new dress shop, the one with the adorable hats."

Distracted, Rebecca found it difficult to concentrate on Sara Jane's chatter. Not for the first time she wondered why everyone was evasive when she questioned setting up a meeting with her father. Taking advantage of the lull in conversation as Sara Jane paused for a breath, Rebecca ventured, "Elizabeth it seems to me, we should have heard something from my father by now. The hearing date is fast approaching. I couldn't help, but wonder if there's something you are not telling me?"

"I will admit we were hoping to spare your feelings to some extent. You appeared to be having such a good time. We wanted to avoid any unpleasantness for as long as possible."

"You are kind to want to protect me. Still, I can withstand whatever you have to say."

Elizabeth's mouth formed a grim line. "Your father believes we are part of some cruel scheme to cause him pain. He holds to his story affirming you are back east at a finishing school. Part of the reason why we are going back to town a little bit prematurely is so we can discuss an idea which could provide additional evidence."

"What kind of evidence?

"We believe it would be beneficial to visit the doctor you saw here in town years ago."

Dumbfounded, Rebecca stared.

Seeing Rebecca's expression, Elizabeth hurried to explain. "Perhaps, if you were examined by the same doctor who treated you as a child, he could confirm your identity rather easily."

Watching Elizabeth's face, Rebecca wondered, if her mother had lived if she would have looked like Elizabeth now. She had been very kind. Even so, could she trust her?

Studying her hand, Rebecca traced the wide ugly scar running through the middle of her palm with her forefinger. It was a reminder of her repeated nightmare of an event that occurred when she lived with her stepmother and of the doctor who treated her. "I only have a vague recollection." Clearing her throat, she said, "I do recall becoming fearful every time I saw him. Dr. Benton mentioned some doctor's methods though acceptable, he considers barbaric. I would prefer not to see the man again."

Elizabeth gasped. "I had no idea. Let's forget I ever suggested anything of the sort."

Rebecca stared into the horizon as she mulled over her childhood. "I have often wondered about my father, questioning why he didn't want me. As a young girl, I would picture him as a character in a fairy tale, a knight in some far away land slaying dragons. As I got older, I believed he was trying to escape the same sort of tragedies we endured, blizzards, locust and the lack of rain. After Papa Horace died, I learned my father was a prosperous rancher, and I quit making excuses."

Elizabeth frowned, blinking rapidly. "Your mother would be so disappointed in your father's actions. Honestly, I would like to throttle the man." Reaching for a handkerchief, she wiped her face.

Rebecca's eyes widened. "Please, don't cry. You caught me feeling a little melancholy. I have had a wonderful life. I was raised by a couple who loved me. I've been surrounded by good friends.

Now, I have y'all and feel more blessed. So please, you must stop," Rebecca pleaded as she fought to keep her own tears from falling.

"You are right, Rebecca. Mama don't cry, or your eyes will be puffy. Then we will have to wait to visit the dress shop," Sara Jane said earnestly.

Elizabeth gasped at her daughter's reaction but upon seeing Rebecca's startled expression, broke out in laughter as Rebecca joined in.

Drawing her mouth into a pout, Sara Jane asked, "Will one of you please tell me what is so funny?"

Chapter 22

Dear Papa,
It is so very cold. Adam says he is afraid that we will lose most of our livestock. Papa Horace doesn't speak of it, but I see him staring out the window. I know that he is worried...

Preparing for church, Rebecca admired
Sara Jane's blue silk dress that perfectly complemented her new hat. It was a beautiful, elaborate design, its brim an overlay aqua silk satin, trimmed with petite silk muslin ruffle and decorated with lace.

Elizabeth had selected a fancy edge, Gable Bonnet, with velvet flowers, trimmed in green ribbon. She insisted Rebecca pick out a new hat also. "It is my treat."

Rebecca hadn't had a new hat in years. She turned the price tag over and gulped. She could feel her eyes widening. "I can't accept this. It's too much."

Elizabeth clucked her tongue as she placed the bonnet on Rebecca's head. "Nonsense, please allow me to do this as back payment for all of those birthdays I missed."

Dressed in her cornflower blue dress this morning, Rebecca admired her reflection in the mirror. She adjusted her hair under the simple straw bonnet trimmed in blue ribbon and flowers quickly before joining her cousins as they made their way to church.

Although she felt a little out of place next to her cousins in their silk dresses, she found her calico dress was more in line with what most of the other women wore at the service. The church was full and warm but pleasant as she benefited from a woman beside her who made good use of her hand-held fan.

Numerous ladybugs flew back and forth as they searched for a place to rest on the sanctuary walls. Despite her best efforts, Rebecca couldn't take her eyes off the tiny red spotted insects. The pastor slapped his hand on the podium which brought her and several others attention back to him.

He held his well-worn Bible out toward the congregation. "This morning we will be discussing how to talk to God, or some would say, approach God in prayer. Turn with me if you will to the Gospel according to Luke, Chapter 11."

"If a son shall ask bread of any of you that is a father, will he give him a stone? Or if he asks for a fish, will he for a fish give him a serpent?"

Thumping the page, he leaned toward the congregation. "God welcomes our prayers, anytime, anywhere, anyhow. He wants to hear from us. He wants to hear from you."

Stepping down from the podium, he paced the front of the church. Thick, dark eyebrows drew together as he studied the faces of the congregation. "Now, let me tell you a story. After being put to bed, a child asked for a drink of water. The father denied the request. The child repeated the question until finally, the father warned if he asked again he was coming to give him a spanking. The child answered, "Pa, when you come to give me my spanking, can you bring a cup of water?"

Chuckling to himself, the pastor pointed his finger at the crowd. "There will be times when we will go through suffering. You might be in a period like that now. If not, hold on, it's coming.

"Though we may never understand why certain things happen, God wants us to talk to him about it in our prayers. We are to trust as a child; knowing if He sees it for our spiritual good it will be granted. Regardless, He will not send us away empty-handed. Let's trust Him today."

Rebecca smiled at Sara Jane as they walked out of the church. "I enjoyed the sermon today. I look forward to sharing the illustration with Pastor Nelson once I get home."

Feeling a little sad, Rebecca realized she was a bit homesick. If she were in Carrie Town today, she would have been leaving the church with Sam. Her shoulders slumped. Although Sam kept his promise about corresponding frequently, she missed him, the girls, Molly, and her family. A small tug on her dress brought her attention back to reality as she was surprised to see Hannah Hood smiling at her.

"Hannah, I am sorry I didn't notice you at first. I had almost forgotten you lived nearby."

Clapping her hands, Hannah hopped up and down. "See Mama. I told you it was Rebecca."

"You sure did. What a nice surprise. Why didn't you tell us you were planning on visiting?"

"At the last minute, I accepted my cousin's invitation." Motioning in the direction of Sara Jane who was chatting happily with a friend, Rebecca continued. "I am staying with the Brooks family. Are you acquainted with them?"

Mary gave a smile and a wave to Sara Jane. "That is Elizabeth Brooks' youngest daughter, isn't it? I daresay it is a small world. Please, step over here for a moment and speak with my father, won't you?"

As they worked their way through the small crowd, Hannah grabbed Rebecca's hand hurrying her along. "Grandfather, Uncle Jacob look, it's Rebecca."

Jonas Weber clasped Rebecca's hand in a warm greeting. "My dear girl, how nice to see you. Miss Towns let me introduce you to my brother, Jacob Weber. He is an attorney here in town. Jacob this is our dear friend, Rebecca, from Carrie Town. She's been a wealth of information and advice regarding our little Hannah."

Rebecca smiled, Examining the two men she at once saw the family resemblance. "Nice to meet you, Mr. Weber."

Jacob Weber stood motionless as introductions were made. "I am sorry young lady. I didn't catch your name. You are a friend of Hannah's, did you say?"

Rebecca felt Sara Jane's hand on her arm. "Excuse me gentlemen, Rebecca, Mama, and Papa are waiting."

Making her excuses, Rebecca hurried away. "It was very nice to meet you. I will see you soon."

Jacob Weber eyed his brother, Jonas, sternly. "Tell me again, what did you say her name was? How do you know her?"

Surprised at her uncle's reaction, Mary volunteered, "She is a patient of Dr. Benton in Carrie Town. He has been treating her for years for the same condition Hannah has. Rebecca is forthcoming and been so helpful about her own struggle with asthma."

"Asthma, you say?"

"Jacob, what in the world has come over you? Why are you acting like this?"

"It is probably a coincidence. Did you say the young lady's last name was Towns?"

"Yes, her name is Rebecca Towns."

Mary placed her hand on her father's sleeve. "Actually, her real name is Rebecca Mueller."

"What?" Both men said simultaneously

Mary Hood patted her father's arm. "Papa, you knew that. You've forgotten. Towns is a nickname she was given when she was a little girl. Her given name is Rebecca Mueller."

Puzzled, Jonas remarked to his daughter, "I don't recall ever hearing her referred to as Mueller."

"It is such a sweet story. You see Rebecca's mother died, and her father couldn't care for her, so the town sort of adopted her."

"How can this be?" Seeing the odd expressions from his brother and niece, Jacob realized he had voiced his thoughts. Tugging at his collar, he continued, "Tell me this Mary, the young lady she was with wouldn't happen to be Elizabeth Brooks' daughter, would she?"

Chapter 23

Dear Papa,
I had a nightmare last night. I dreamed I was so hot that I couldn't breathe. When I woke up the scar on my hand was itching...

Adam tried to keep a straight face as he observed the uneaten roast left on the table. "Emma let me take those leftovers to Cookie. I bet the ranch hands will finish it off in no time."

"Really? I didn't think it was any good. There was so much left."

"Don't be silly, your cooking is coming along fine. I filled up on potato soup. Did I mention how good the bread was? It was delicious."

Emma searched her father's face. "Pa, you aren't just saying that are you? If it wasn't for Molly, I would have burned the soup too."

Adam glanced at the ceiling as he contemplated what he could truthfully say without hurting his daughter's feelings. He glanced over at Grace and

Sadie who had remained unexpectedly quiet while drying the dishes.

Both girls eyed the leftovers of overdone meat but catching his meaning Grace offered a smile of encouragement. "Aunt Molly said you are coming right along on your cooking. You get a little better each day, right Sadie?"

Sadie's forehead puckered. "It's true…she did say that." Wavering she added, "The bread was good. Especially after you cut the burnt parts off."

Adam winked at the girls. "See there. You are doing fine. It simply takes practice. Now you go take a break or go out to your garden which I know you've been itching to do. We will make sure everything gets cleaned up, won't we, girls?"

Emma eyed the girls suspiciously before bolting out the door.

Adam motioned for Grace to help him clear the food off the table. "Let's put this food in something so Emma won't see. Sadie, you keep watch. Let us know if she heads back this way".

The threesome worked together until Adam placed the last of the food into a flour sack. "Now not a word you two. If I hear you squealed, I'm liable to make you eat whatever Emma makes from this point on."

Heeding the warning, solemnly both girls agreed. Grace nudged Sadie with her elbow. "Don't worry she won't hear anything from us, we promise."

"Alright now, you girls know I don't want to hurt her feelings, right? We know how much she hates cooking, but we appreciate her pitching in and doing her best. Now I am going out to the barn to see if I can get some of your pa's shepherds to eat this."

Sadie gasped. "Uncle Adam, please don't, it might kill them."

Laughing as he picked up the sack, he shook his head and headed for the barn. Adam motioned for Sam as he carried the bag over to the shepherd who had recently delivered a litter of pups. "Sam, alright if I give your mama dog some of the leftover roast?"

Not hesitating at all, Sam replied, "You can sure offer it to her, but I doubt she will eat it."

Laughing together, they watched as the dog finished the roast off appreciatively.

Adam grinned from ear to ear. "What do you know about that? She polished it off in no time."

Sam shuddered. "Better her than me."

Chuckling, Adam agreed. "I sure thought Emma would have gotten a handle on this cooking thing by now. I will be glad when Molly is better or when Rebecca gets back."

Sam pulled a letter from his pocket and showed it to Adam. "It seems it might be a while. Sounds as though her pa is putting up a stink. He seems determined to prove Rebecca is an imposter. She mentioned she might have to get another doctor to examine her to compare her medical records. I don't like the sound of it. I wish she would give up on the whole thing."

"I understand how you feel. Even so, I think it is important Rebecca see this through. I noticed you talking to Peter earlier today, what did he have to say?"

Sam motioned his head at the house. "I wanted to wait to discuss it when there were no little ears to hear."

"We probably have a few minutes. After the girls get through with their chores, they were going to sit with Molly. She' been reading *Little Women* to them again. I don't know how many times she's read it. Still, they can't seem to hear it often enough. I believe I can about recite it from memory myself."

Sam surveyed the exterior of the house to confirm the girls had not ventured outside. "Peter doesn't seem surprised in the least by what is going on. I can't understand a man acting in that way toward his own daughter. Peter said Rebecca's father raised his stepchildren in a privileged lifestyle. He has two sons by the second wife to boot. All accounts say he is an attentive father."

Adam shook his head. "I have been scratching my head over that man's actions for years."

"Peter did say Rebecca was taking things in stride. He said she has put on weight and seems to be enjoying her stay. Every time I think about how I ignored what she was going through it makes me sick to my stomach."

"You can't go back and undo anything, all you can do is do better going forward. Other than going to fetch Rebecca back, what do you feel you could or should do for her straightaway?"

"I've been thinking. I want to be there when she meets with her father."

"Do it then."

"Would you and Emma be willing to watch the girls for me for a week or two? I hate to ask, especially since Molly is having so much trouble."

Smiling at the thought of his wife who had been bored to tears since the doctor told her to stay in bed for at least the next few months, Adam agreed. "Molly is fine. Doc says if we can keep her in bed a little longer she should be able to make it almost full term. She is fed up with all the resting and worried too. The girls won't let her be bored, that is for sure. Besides her mother will be coming to help any day now. So, we will have plenty of help."

As a weight of concern lifted, Sam sighed in relief. "If you are certain it is okay? I will take the order I just finished to get it ready to ship. While I'm in town, I will stop by Peter's office to take him up on his offer to let me go along with him next week. Sam motioned to the saddle on his workbench. While I am visiting Rebecca, I will deliver Mr. Weber's saddle personally."

Winking, Adam replied, "Sounds like a mighty good plan."

Chapter 24

Dear Papa,
Adam said I could live with him and Molly forever if need be. I don't feel right about it though…

Standing in his attorney's office, Charles Mueller swiped his large hand through his blonde hair now streaked with silver and shouted, "That's a lie, who put you up to this?"

As a private investigator John Cumming was familiar with delivering, news people didn't want to receive. He was highly recommended, his reputation stellar and his services came at no small cost. He waited for an affirmative nod from Jacob Weber, the attorney, before proceeding.

"Mr. Mueller, don't you think given the fact there was a substantial bonus to disprove the original report I would have done so? There is not, nor has there ever been a Rebecca or Becky Mueller at the school she was to have attended.

Additionally, there is no administrator at the school by the name you provided who sent the quarterly reports."

"Whoever has been dispersing the money has been getting away with it for years. As a result, your daughter has not been provided for. Not only has she never attended school back east, she is currently staying here in town."

"Bah, what you have seen is one of Elizabeth Brooks' daughters. If I didn't know it myself, I could see how they could be mistaken for Leah's child. Taking out his pocket watch, Charles gazed at a photo. "My wife and her cousin were very similar in appearance."

He heaved a sigh and nodded his head. "Yes, they are all lovely. I have seen them all together recently at a local social. Let me say your daughter is a very petite version of her cousins."

Charles's gaze jumped to his, his eyes widening. The investigator had finally gotten his attention. Becky had always been small. Could this be true? Shaking his head, he said, "I will not be pulled into this madness."

"Again, Mr. Mueller, you paid me to do a job. I did it. If you would like, I could do some additional investigation on your bookkeeper. If you would allow me to see his ledger, it's possible we could get to the bottom of this quickly."

After being met with a stony silence, the investigator continued, "No matter what course of action is taken, you have your report. I am grieved to present it as I would have liked to have earned that bonus."

Putting on his hat to leave he paused. "You haven't asked for my advice, Mr. Mueller. Nonetheless, I will give it to you. If it were me, I would be hightailing it to the Brooks home where I would beg on bended knee for my daughter to forgive me. From all accounts, she is both kind and compassionate. Maybe, she will give you a chance to make it up to her."

"You are right on one thing Mr. Cumming, I didn't ask for your advice."

"I will bid you good day sir. Feel free to contact me if you ever have need of my services or if you have any questions about the report."

Jacob Weber waited patiently for a response before finally breaking the silence, "Charles, as you are aware, our court hearing is approaching. This is the third report that brought the same results. My own brother has been acquainted with Rebecca while she lived in Carrie Town these last several years. Perhaps it might be in everyone's best interest to meet with her personally. The Brooks family has certainly offered to bring her to meet with you on a number of occasions."

"Bah. I told you what I think of Elizabeth Brooks. None of this is true. I am sure of it."

"This is certainly beyond anything I could imagine. Nevertheless, the facts are stacking up against us. Which leads me again to this question, what if your daughter is here in town waiting to meet you? Do you actually want to meet her as an oppositional force in court?"

"My opinion is unchanged, Jacob. She is not my daughter. I have wired my business partner. I asked him to return as soon as possible. He should be able to give us the information to disprove all of this. I expect you to represent me to that effect."

Chapter 25

Dear Papa,
Papa Horace passed away today. Even though he tried to prepare me, I didn't handle it well. I cried so hard. I lost my breath. It has been years since I have had an attack. My heart is broken. Please come...

Waiting at the train station, Rebecca stared excitedly at the tracks for the past due train. Elizabeth wanted to let Sam's visit be a surprise; however, Sara Jane had not been able to keep the secret. She fretted over Rebecca all morning and coaxed her to wear her hair down under her new bonnet. She had been happy with her appearance and laughed at Sara Jane's comment that they could be twins.

Sara Jane waved her fan. "Mama, what time did they say the train would arrive? It is so hot out here."

Rebecca had come to love her cousins. She

watched as Elizabeth glanced at her heart-shaped watch pinned to her dress and admired her firm but patient response to her daughter. "Settle down Sara Jane, it should be any minute now."

"Look, Rebecca, I believe I see smoke. Yes, it is the train. Isn't it Mama? Oh, I am so excited."

Elizabeth shook her head at her daughter. "If I didn't know better I would say we were here to meet *your* beau, Sara Jane."

"Oh, Mama. I am excited for Rebecca. After all, as much as we have heard about Sam. I feel as though he is an old friend."

Sara Jane squeezed Rebecca's arm. "Aren't you excited? 'Not waiting for a response, she continued, "I know you must be."

Rebecca felt her stomach churning. She tried to moisten her lips, but her mouth was as dry as sawdust. "It's probably best I do not get my hopes up. Sam is busy and can't afford to take this much time off from work." Sweat broke across her forehead as she watched as passengers began to disembark. Finally, she saw the familiar figure of Peter, striding purposely in their direction. Feeling her lips quiver, she looked away, trying not to show her disappointment.

Sara Jane elbowed Rebecca. "Take a look at him, why don't you?"

Glancing in the direction where Sara Jane motioned, Rebecca saw a muscular cowboy with a saddle draped over one shoulder, carrying a tote in his other arm. His blue shirt and vest hinted at broad shoulders and narrow waist.

Sara Jane whispered. "Isn't he handsome?"

"I don't see how you would know if he is handsome," Rebecca countered, "between his hat and saddle …"

As soon as the word saddle was out of her mouth, Rebecca stared. Feeling the familiar squeeze on her elbow, she turned again. "Sara Jane, I can't hear out of that ear, what is it you are saying?"

Attempting to be inconspicuous, Sara Jane tipped her head slightly. "Could that be…"

Rebecca gasped. "Sam."

Shifting the weight of his saddle, Sam turned toward the sound of her voice with a furrowed brow as he searched the crowded boardwalk.

Feeling a little bolder, she stepped forward, calling his name again. Recognition crossed his face as he pushed his way through the crowd. "Becca, honey, I walked right past you. I guess I didn't recognize you in your new hat." Placing the saddle at his feet, he took her hand and brought it to his lips. "You are a sight for sore eyes, for sure. I missed you so much."

Blushing, she said, "I saw Peter but didn't see you. I was afraid you weren't coming."

Sighing, he squeezed her hand. "I'm sorry I worried you. I would have sent word ahead of time if I weren't going to make it." Sam leaned forward and winked. "Trust me. Wild horses couldn't have kept me away."

Sara Jane elbowed Rebecca again. "Aren't you going to introduce me?

Rebecca, filled with relief, laughed as she grabbed Sara Jane's arm to prevent any further assault on her ribs. "Sam let me introduce you to my cousin, Sara Jane. "Sara Jane, this is Sam."

Sara Jane responded in her best southern drawl, a smile and a twirl of her parasol. "Indeed, it is a pleasure."

With a slight rise to the eyebrows and a teasing grin, Sam turned to Rebecca. "Let me store this saddle and then why don't we go get something to eat? I don't know about you ladies, but I am starving".

"Now don't you worry about dinner, Mama has everything taken care of. We are going to eat at our house in town. She's waiting for us over there with the attorney. Rebecca tells me you like fried chicken. Our cook is trying to teach her, did she tell you?"

As Sara Jane prattled on, Sam offered his arm and leaned closer to Rebecca. He whispered. "Does she ever stop talking?"

Shaking her head in response, they laughed softly together as Sara Jane continued her one-way conversation. Feeling the warmth of Sam's arm as he held her hand in the crook of his, Rebecca could still hardly believe he was here. As she silently prayed her thanks to God, she felt genuinely content for the first time in years.

Chapter 26

Dear Papa,
Mr. Marks offered me a job at his law office. I will be going to stay in town at the boarding house until I hear from you. Please come...

Charles Mueller walked through the front door of his home searching for his wife. Finding no signs of her, he motioned for his stepson Robert. "I am assuming James has not arrived, so bring the accounting ledger. You and I are going to go over it line by line."

Charles opened the door to the office he shared with James Taylor, his friend, business partner, and accountant for the past twelve years. He was a relative of his wife, and she pressured him to give him a chance. Charles had been hesitant about hiring him but desperate to find an accountant that could work with his wife, had given him the job.

Surprisingly, the two forged a friendship. James proved his worth many times over by implementing improvements that produced solid profits. It was James who suggested they purchase more hay for the winter. Advice Charles had half-heartedly taken. However, his instinct was correct, and they were able to avoid catastrophe. James, again, suggested he hire drovers to bring cattle to Kansas.

Traveling ten to fifteen miles a day slowly driving the cattle to market, Charles had eaten a daily diet of coffee, beef, beans, biscuits, and dust. Financially, it was all worth it. The last few years the need to drive cattle was no longer necessary as they were able to ship by rail to the nearby slaughterhouses.

An added benefit was the additional time at home allowed him the opportunity to pour his life into his two young sons, who were now eleven and six. Much to their mother's vexation, they loved ranching almost as much as he did.

Hearing a door slam, Charles rose to investigate and was met by his stepdaughter Lucy, loaded with packages. Clearing his throat, he said, "Lucy, I believe I made my feelings clear on the extent of your shopping trips. You have not remained within budget the last six months. There seems to be no end to your extravagance. I am putting my foot down. Whatever those packages are, unless it is produce for our pantry, turn around and take it back."

"Papa, you startled me. I didn't expect you to be here today."

"I can see you are surprised."

"Mama wanted me to have these things for my birthday party. Besides, I can't take them back."

"Why?"

"Mama insisted on certain things, and everything was tailored specifically for me. I simply can't return anything."

"Very well. However, I am warning you, young lady, as I see I have no choice but to go into the shops personally. The shopkeepers will be told they are not to accept any orders on credit from either of you. You would be wise not to treat this as an idle threat. This will not be the first time I have visited the merchants regarding your mother's shopping habits."

"Papa, how embarrassing. I can't believe you would do that to me." Crying, Lucy ran up the stairs to her room, slamming the door.

Exasperated, he turned back to the office where his stepson Robert was waiting.

Although both Robert and Lucy inherited their mother's dark hair and brown eyes, that is where the similarity ended. Robert was the opposite in personality. He was quiet, considerate, displayed a good work ethic and never asked for anything, preferring to make his own way.

"Pa, I have been examining these books over the last week. Admittedly, I am at my wit's end to balance anything related to the household expenses. I took the liberty of searching through James' desk when I remembered he told me Mother handled the household expenditures."

Charles watched Robert stack journals with receipts and small items of paper protruding from their binding.

"I rue the day I agreed to let your mother have

her own personal account," Charles said. Grimacing, he thought back on what torture each month brought and the many hours he spent with Louisa stressing the importance of making note of each expenditure. She inevitably would break down in tears, crying and complaining. "Why it's none of their business what I buy and for whom or for what. Am I your wife or a servant?"

Wanting to put a stop to her nagging, reluctantly he'd agreed to set up an account for Louisa with specific amounts each month for household items, clothes, and entertainment. It was a budget she treated with total disregard and another source of irritation which strained their relationship.

Charles smiled at Robert, who looked embarrassed by the state of his mother's bookkeeping. "Yes, your mother, much to my irritation, handles all of the household expenses. How she handles them is another matter. What does this have to do with the monies related to my daughter?"

Robert searched through the pile and pulled out several items. "There is a memo written by James and initialed by you as authorization for any funds related to Becky to be paid from the household account."

Looking at his stepfather, he proceeded. "From a bookkeeping standpoint, it makes sense, to have the household expense separate from the ranch. Since Mother has overseen those expenditures, it is challenging to make sense of the records. From what I can tell, she overspent her budget each month in excessive amounts."

Charles sighed. While he ran a profitable business, Robert's mother and sister's extravagant lifestyle had been a constant strain on his budget.

Robert took a deep breath. "Pa, when my mother married you, it was the best thing that ever happened to me. You have been a father to me, and I am more grateful than you will ever know."

Swallowing and motioning at the general disarray of his mother's accounts, he continued, "But based on what I have been able to determine through these records, Becky hasn't been provided for financially—in years."

Slamming his hands on his desk, Charles growled. "I am sick to death of hearing this. Am I the kind of man who would not support my own child? I would never disrespect my wife's memory in that way. My daughter has been my driving force to make a success of the ranch. I wanted to fulfill the dream Leah and I had for Becky and what we hoped would be a house full of our children."

Stopping, Charles took a moment to gather his thoughts. "Robert, I mean no disrespect to you, in this. You have been a source of pleasure for me and would make any man proud to call you son. I care for you no less than I do your brothers, Charlie and Mark."

Charles reached for his pocket watch, not to check the time, but in fact to gaze at the photo of his first wife and child. "When James gets back he will be able to clear this up, I am sure."

"I hope so. I truly do. If not, I promise you, I will find a way to pay this all back."

"What?" Feeling his gut wrench, Charles

continued almost hesitantly, "Robert, it is not like you to be dramatic. What have you found?"

Taking his handkerchief, Robert wiped the sweat from his brow as he reached for his notes. "Maybe, it will be best if I start by showing you how I have come to this conclusion. I can only pray there are some facts you might add which will disprove my theory."

Chapter 27

Dear Papa,
Mr. Marks told me today that you sent all of my letters back without reading them. Molly thought it might make me feel better to write my thoughts down. I am reluctant to do so because Aunt Eloise taught me to mind my tongue. I feel confident she would not encourage me to put pen to paper in this case...

Sam took Rebecca's hand and leaned forward. "Whatever you want is fine by me. I will support your decision. If at any point you decide all of this is too much, I will respect that. Either way, I want to be by your side."

Elizabeth smiled at Sam yet watched Rebecca with concern. "I keep hoping the worst is behind us."

Not trusting her voice to remain steady, Rebecca tried to maintain a calm appearance. She was relieved to see the door open as the doctor entered the office.

"Hello again young lady. I see you have brought some additional reinforcement," he said, chuckling at his attempt to lighten the mood. "Now, let's get down to brass tacks, shall we? I found your case fascinating. Especially as it relates to your physicians who took an opposite approach to your treatment."

Dr. Ziegler removed his eyeglasses and began polishing them distractedly as he reviewed Rebecca's patient file. "I believe Dr. Benton's approach not only saved your life but allowed you to lead what most would see as a normal life with little impediment."

"From a physician's viewpoint, based on the reports of your physical condition when you were a patient of Dr. Duran's, my professional opinion would have been you would not survive childhood."

Elizabeth gasped, and Rebecca felt Sam stiffen. However, she was not surprised by the doctor's assessment. Sam having recovered his composure, grinned and commented, "Doc, if you knew how stubborn she is, you wouldn't have been surprised at all."

Dr. Ziegler laughed, nodding in agreement. "Call it what you will—stubbornness, luck, grit, or the hand of God, statistics would suggest you beat the odds, young lady. The reason I say this is simply to make you aware your current state of good health would be enough to make one question whether you could possibly be the same Rebecca Mueller treated all those years ago. However, there are a few specific facts I think should be brought to the forefront."

Taking her hand and turning it over, he remarked, "Your chart indicates more than 15 stitches on the palm of your right hand. You have a scar on the same hand matching the description. Do you remember how you received the injury?"

Uncomfortable, Rebecca retrieved her trembling hand and placed it on her lap.

Sensing her distress, Sam whispered, "Rebecca honey, you don't have to do this. Give me the word, then you and I will walk out of here."

Rebecca took a deep breath then shook her head. "No, I want to answer. I do have some memory of how it happened as well as reoccurring nightmares over the years."

"Tell me what you can remember," the doctor urged.

"When I went to live with my father after he remarried, my stepsister and I did not get along. She was given the bedroom my mother decorated for me. I hated everything about my new room, since it was small, hot, and the window was nailed shut. I was angry. I remember telling my stepmother, Lucy shouldn't be there and she should be given the smaller room."

"There was never a moment's peace between Lucy and me. I was miserable. I spent most of my time in the kitchen with the cook, trying to avoid Lucy. It was the one area in the house she avoided. One of the last days I remember living at the ranch, my father saw Lucy teasing me about my ragdoll. He made her give me one of her fancy ceramic dolls to play with. When I woke up the next day, my ragdoll's hair had been cut off. I was furious and stormed into Lucy's room while she was still in bed and well...I whaled into her. She denied any wrongdoing and went crying to her mother."

"As punishment, I was sent to my room for the day without breakfast. I didn't mind at first, but my room was so hot. I banged on the door to be let out. No one came. I tried to open the window, and when I looked out, I saw my stepbrother Robby outside. I kept yelling and banging on the window trying to get his attention. The glass broke. The next thing I remember was that my hand was bleeding."

The sound of a muttered curse caused her to look at Sam whose jaw was clenched in fury.

"I vaguely recall someone calling to me and breaking the door in. When I woke, I felt as though someone was sitting on my chest. It was difficult to breathe."

"Yes, Dr. Duran noted you were in a state of respiratory distress when he arrived. His treatment for you was chloroform. The theory is when taken in small doses it will relax muscles and induce sleep, and upon waking your asthma attack would have ceased."

"Many others in our profession at the time—and some still do—believe the influence of the mind causes asthma. A psychological problem brought on by strong emotions, such as anxiety or excessive sadness such as the yearning for the mother. You certainly were under stress, and of course, you'd lost your mother the previous year. Therefore, it would be a logical conclusion. His recommendations included a regiment of bleeding and emetics to induce vomiting."

Elizabeth took Rebecca's hand and asked gently, "Where was your father at this time, do you recall?"

"He was there at one point. I remember my stepmother saying I was disrupting everything to get attention. He spanked me and told me to take my medicine and quit coughing. He held me while my stepmother forced me to drink the medicine. Afterward, I remember trying not to cry or cough." Pausing for a moment, she looked directly at Elizabeth. "Then I vomited all over my father's boots."

A small giggle erupted from Elizabeth, who immediately apologized profusely. "Rebecca, I am so sorry. I know how particular your father is about his boots. But, I can't help but think well done."

Elizabeth's comment brought a brief chuckle to everyone, including the doctor. "I believe laughter is good for the soul. In all seriousness, after this asthma attack, you contracted pneumonia. Your prognosis was noted as grim. Between the bleeding, and the emetics it is my opinion, surprising you survived."

Doctor Duran's recommendation states he felt it would be better for you to recover in a calm environment without the additional stress of a stepmother and step-siblings. Based on what you told us, I wholeheartedly agree."

Placing his glasses back across his nose, Doctor Ziegler paused for a moment as he examined additional notes. "There are some other transcripts I believe it is important to share. Your doctor at the time recommended institutionalization. Your stepmother agreed. The records say your father rejected the idea in a very hostile manner."

Tapping his pencil on the document, looking directly into Rebecca's eyes, he emphasized. "The word hostile is underlined three times. The final decision was for you to be placed in the care of Mr. and Mrs. Phillips. Dr. Duran noted a loving home would be advantageous to an institution. However, his concern was the age of the caretakers. Your father agreed to provide domestic help and cover all expenses. You, of course, recovered, except for the loss of hearing, which was believed to be caused by the high fever during your bout with pneumonia."

"Now, to get back to the business at hand, my opinion will be based on my examination of you, the reports from both doctors and your recollection of the facts. I will be issuing a statement that in my professional opinion, you are the same child, now grown woman known as Rebecca, "Becky," Mueller. I would be happy to testify in a court of law, should it be necessary."

As they left the office, Sam stopped to shake Dr. Ziegler's hand.

"Much obliged, Doc. I think you have helped more than you can imagine. This is the first time Rebecca's been made aware of what actions her father took toward her care. I can't imagine what I would have done in the same situation. Even so, I am still worried if I ever see the man in person, it will be all I can do to keep from punching him square in the mouth."

Chapter 28

Dear Papa,
Molly is correct. It does make me feel better to write my thoughts down. The fact that you will never read these words perhaps gives me the courage to say what I really think…

Hearing the conductor announce the next stop, James Taylor swiped his hair with his hand for a quick comb and rose to leave. His trip back east to negotiate with another meatpacking distributor had been profitable. However, the repeated telegraphs had him worried.

Charles was a hard taskmaster but generally allowed him time to finish a job without interference. After more than three weeks away, he wanted very much to go home, greet the family, and rest. As he exited the train to claim his baggage, he was brought up short by the voice of Charles Mueller. "Thank God you are here, James. I need your help."

"I received the telegraphs yesterday. I came straight away. I must tell you I am more than a little tired. The meetings went fine by the way."

With a pat on his back, Charles steered James in the direction of the boardwalk. "I expected nothing less. However, this is a personal matter. Can you come with me now to my attorney's office? Robert is here. He will see to your belongings."

James found it strange Charles wished to speak about something personal. While their relationship was a good one, it was strictly business. They enjoyed lively discussions, geared to the price of cattle, grain or ideas on increasing profits. He doubted Charles would be familiar enough with his personal life to even know his children's names.

James matched Charles' strides as they made their way in silence. Upon arrival, they were immediately ushered into the office of Jacob Weber who made quick work of explaining the situation.

James rubbed his chin in contemplation. "When I first was offered this job, it was with the understanding I was to handle the business affairs. I would only transfer funds into the household account as approved by Charles or you, Mr. Weber. It was made clear to me Louisa wanted to take care of the household financials without my help."

Jacob Weber rose from his chair to retrieve another file. "James, where does the request for payments come from? Are you provided with invoices?"

"No, I am given a list from Louisa each quarter as to what the expenses are. From the beginning, I was directed not to insist on invoices. But I required was to provide an itemized statement, even if it meant I was to write the list myself."

"Are you familiar with the bookkeeper who distributes the funds? Have you ever done business with him before?"

"Yes, he was hired by Louisa when Charles arranged a separate account for household expenses. He pays the bills. She seems happy with the arrangement. His information is back at the office."

Charles looked grim as he moved to sit in the chair closest to James. "Robert found the name and address of the bookkeeper. He sent a wire asking him to meet with us. He is at the train station waiting for him now."

Charles rubbed his temples and stared off in the distance. "It was a mistake to marry so quickly after Leah's death. But I was lonely. I believed my daughter needed a mother. Louisa was beautiful and so different from my first wife, I was intrigued and grabbed at a chance for happiness again. I was delighted with both of her children. I assumed they would be wonderful playmates for Becky."

"When I arrived home after the roundup, everything was in chaos. My wife blamed my daughter, saying she was spoiled. I have since seen how Louisa's affection is devoted exclusively to Lucy. She demands the same level of attention from everyone. I don't know if what I could provide was not enough, or if she simply could not abide the fact my daughter might receive something Lucy might want."

James countered, "But Charles, I understood that Becky is attending finishing school. Surely, she could not be attending such a school without your financial support?"

"We have been provided with information confirming my daughter never attended such a school and is in fact here in town, staying with the Brooks family."

Jacob Weber took this moment to interject, "The physician confirmed her identity based on physical evidence and her recollection of certain events. Those happenings have been validated as having taken place."

"Since I was not there at the time of the accident, I was led to believe a different story of how Becky came to be injured. Robert confirmed her recollections are true. Although I wish to God, it was not so."

A strained silence took place as all three men tried to come to grips with the depths of the deception. The silence was interrupted by a knock on the door followed by the arrival of Louisa's bookkeeper.

Chapter 29

Dear Papa,
I turned 17 today. Mrs. Potts gave me time off, so I could spend the day with Molly...

With a satisfied look, as her recent purchases were loaded into the front hall, Louisa Mueller entered her home displaying a triumphant smile, calling for her daughter.

Charles Mueller motioned to his housekeeper. "Don't bother having any of those packages sent up to Lucy. They will all be going back to wherever they came from."

Louisa gasped. "Charles, you are early."

"Yes, earlier than expected. I imagine you planned to have everything put away before my arrival."

Louisa narrowed her eyes at her husband. "Whatever is the matter with you? These are simply a few things we will need for Lucy's birthday celebration."

"The few", he said raising his eyebrows, "will be returned. Now wife, if you will join me in my office, we have much to discuss."

Louisa waved her hand in dismissal. "I am certainly not going to participate in another lecture on the importance of following a budget. I do my best with the meager funds you give me. You should try to run a household on what you allot."

Charles' eyes smoldered. He pointed at the door, shouting. "Now, Louisa."

Louisa changed tactics, taking his arm. "Charles, really it is not like you to carry on so, especially in front of the domestic staff. If Lucy overspent, it is because she is excited about her birthday party."

Charles studied his wife. He couldn't help but notice how lovely she was, especially when she attempted to be pleasant. "Enough, no more about your shopping, your spending, your parties. I have been a fool; however, a veil has been lifted from my eyes. I now see who you are, what you have done. I know it all."

Louisa smiled coyly. "Charles, how mysterious you are. I have already apologized for Lucy's overspending. We can subtract whatever the amount is from next month's budget."

Charles picked up his accounting ledger, turning the pages. "Yes, I see. Simply make a note of the expense so you can debit it from my daughter's allowance. That is the reason for going over budget each month, isn't it? If your account is overdrawn, then you do not have the money necessary to make a transfer."

Louisa headed for a mirror and adjusted her hair. Their eyes locked as she admired her reflection. "Exactly what are you accusing me of, Charles?"

"Louisa, your day of reckoning is today. You are a liar and a thief."

She turned to exit the room. "I am not going to sit here and listen to this. Go back to the ranch you love so much. Leave me here in peace."

Charles reached for Louisa's arm and stopped her retreat. "Nothing would make you happier than to be left to yourself, to do as you will. My dear wife, those days are over."

Louisa pulled her arm from his grasp. "Have you run mad? What are you about?"

Charles tapped the ledger with a loud thump. "Although, I will take my share of the blame. I will not allow you to continue your games. I have spoken to your bookkeeper. I have all the records. The legal term, of course, is embezzlement."

Louisa crossed her arms and shrugged. "I have simply been using our own money. If you hadn't been so stingy with my allowance, I would never have gone to such extremes. Besides, what does a child like that need money? Why does she deserve it over our other children?"

"Whether you believe she deserves it or not, the money used to purchase the ranch was a gift to my wife, from her grandfather. As you well know, the stipulation to the inheritance is the original acreage for the ranch, the house the livestock, percentage of profits, all of it, will belong to Becky."

Charles took in a deep breath, exhaling slowly.

"Which is why I have worked so hard to be able to purchase more acreage, so the boys could have a good start on a ranch of their own. Other profits put aside, are only a small portion of what you have stolen."

Louisa tilted her head and raised one eyebrow. "Stolen?" I have earned it."

Charles jaw dropped. "Have you no soul, woman? You deceived me all these years. Denied me access to my daughter, when I have taken your children in and loved them?"

"Love, is that what you call it?"

Charles' eyes narrowed. "My definition is different from yours. But, yes. I believe you substitute the meaning of love with possessions."

Louisa pressed her finger into her husband's chest. "Oh, let's bring Lucy into this, shall we? You never loved my daughter. I had to do something to make it up to her. Besides the only thing you ever cared about was your obsession with your dead wife and her child."

Charles gritted his teeth. "Have I ever denied you anything? Do you think if you had been honest with me about your children's trust fund, I would not have paid for their education?"

Louisa's finger absently traced the blue opal glass oil lamp. "You would not have paid for where I wanted to send them. I did what I needed to do to allow them to attend a school worthy of them."

"What of Becky, did she deserve no less?"

"Becky is not my concern."

"Yes, you have made your feelings abundantly clear. "

Louisa lifted her chin. "I will sue you for divorce."

"On what grounds?"

Louisa forced her mouth into a pout. "Cruelty."

Charles barked with laughter. "Cruelty? Look at this house, at your clothes. You have been denied nothing."

"You never loved me."

"And you never loved me. We married to help each other with our children, to combat our loneliness. I hoped we might grow to love one another or at least to be content. I have tried my best to live up to my side of the bargain."

"You have no love left for me because it was all buried in the grave of your first wife."

"Did you not tell me you felt the same about your first husband?"

Louisa shrugged before placing both hands on her hips. "I will not cancel Lucy's party. Everything has been ordered. Most of it paid for."

Charles rolled his eyes. "That is what you are concerned about, Lucy's party? What about my daughter who never so much as received a new dress or a pair of shoes from her father?"

"She belongs in an institution. It would be a waste of effort to send her anything of value."

Charles opened and closed his fists as he stared at his wife. Her beautiful face twisted in fury. "That was not your decision to make. My lawyer will contact you with details on some sort of settlement. If it were not for the children, I would be tempted to have you thrown in jail. So, don't fight me on this Louisa. The more money we get from the sale of this house, the more likely there will be enough funds to set you up somewhere else. Perhaps, you can go back east to live with your sister. You have threatened me with doing so often enough."

Charles walked over to his safe. "I will leave you with a small amount of cash, but no more. Additionally, all of the merchants here in town have been told not to extend you credit."

Louisa picked up a vase and hurled it across the room at Charles.

Dodging, he said, "That was an expensive vase was it not? Again, I warn you any settlement you may receive will come *after* the sale of this house. You might want to consider the cost before you throw anything else."

Chapter 30

Dear Papa,
Although the boarding house is almost always full and very noisy, it is so lonely living in town…

Darkness filled the room. Rebecca tossed the quilt aside, sweating profusely, and sat on the side of the bed. Rising to open the window, she allowed the breeze to cool her as she took in deep breaths. *Was it the heat of the night or the memories of her childhood that had caused a reoccurrence of the old familiar nightmare?* Glancing at the rumpled sheets, she decided to allow herself some time to calm down before attempting to go back to sleep. She quietly strolled into the parlor and opened her Bible to locate a favorite verse.

Colossians 3:13 'Bearing with one another, and forgiving one another if anyone has a complaint against another; even as Christ forgave you, so you also must do."

Suddenly, memories of her disastrous first day

at school flooded her mind. The pastor stopped by to make sure Rebecca was on her way to recovery. Although she experienced waves of dizziness and nausea, during the first several days after the incident, she recovered. Fearful of triggering another episode, she had sequestered herself in the bed.

Horace made no pretense of hiding his anger with her childhood friend, B.J. She had heard him voice his concerns to Pastor Nelson. "I know the boy feels bad. But she was so excited about starting school. Now she is afraid to get out of bed."

Later, the pastor visited with Rebecca and read from the book of Exodus of how Moses led the people out of Egypt. She recalled imagining she was one of the hundreds of thousands of people who left Egypt in the middle of the night, walking through the desert toward the Red Sea.

Pastor Nelson explained how the Israelites were trapped. To the east was the sea, to the south and west were mountains and to the north was Pharaoh's army. But God would provide a miracle so great all of Egypt would know He was Lord. "Do you think the Israelites were afraid?"

"I bet they were shaking in their boots," Rebecca answered solemnly.

Pastor Nelson chuckled. "The Israelites were afraid and blamed Moses for being trapped. Even so, God told Moses to hold out his staff, to reach his hand over the Red Sea which would part the water and allow the people to cross. Then He gave the Israelites a pillar of clouds to lead them during the day and a pillar of fire at night. He did this because he wanted it to serve as a reminder that God was always with them guiding them."

Rebecca smiled as she recalled asking why God hadn't sent her a cloud as a guide. Pastor Nelson explained how God gave us something the Israelites didn't have, the Bible and the Holy Spirit. "The Bible is God's Word, and it reassures us He is with us day and night."

Rebecca turned to the passage in Romans chapter 8:14-17. 'For all who are led by the Spirit of God are children of God. So, you have not received a spirit that makes you fearful slaves. Instead, you received God's Spirit when he adopted you as his own children. Now we call him, "Abba, Father."

She used her finger to trace the note placed by Pastor Nelson, "When you are afraid to trust in God." *Alright, God, I am trusting.*

Startled by a noise, Rebecca looked into the eyes of Elizabeth who was holding a tray of milk and cookies. "I didn't mean to scare you. I thought you heard me come in."

Laughing softly as she held her hand over her heart, Rebecca breathed in and out as she willed her pulse to slow down from her brief shock. "Only this minute, I was talking to God about being afraid."

Elizabeth grinned, I have heard it said that God's timing is perfect. It seems mine is not. I didn't mean to frighten you."

Still feeling her heart race, Rebecca took in a deep breath. "I had a troubling dream and decided to read for a while before I tried to go back to sleep."

"It worried me when you spoke to the doctor

about having nightmares. I was hoping that was something in the past tense." Elizabeth patted Rebecca's hand then placed the cookies between them. "No matter what troubles me, I find something sweet helps me to have a different outlook on things."

Rebecca bit into a cookie and closed her eyes, savoring the sweetness. "I believe your method might cause me to want to have a bad dream, so I can have a midnight treat."

Elizabeth nodded. "I am sure your technique is superior. Do you mind sharing what you are reading?"

Rebecca slid the Bible closer. "No matter how many times I look at it, it seems to say something to different to me each time."

Looking over her shoulder, Elizabeth read the passage. "Does the verse speak to you because it reminds you we have a Father in heaven who loves you? Or is it the reference to fear?"

"Both I guess. Since my parents did not raise me, I was often reminded that I was a child of God. This verse was something our pastor used to encourage me, after a painful event on my first day of school. The funny thing is now when I think about what happened I laugh."

Seeing the puzzlement on Elizabeth's face, Rebecca explained about her problems with vertigo and how a childhood friend spun her around to cure her. "It seems silly now, but it comes to mind because I was angry with a friend and afraid to get out of bed. My pastor was the one who finally convinced me to let go of my fears and forgive my friend."

Rebecca moved her finger along the underlined words in her Bible. "When I read this verse as an adult, I am ashamed I have been feeling sorry for myself. Even though I wish things were different, I had a wonderful life. I have a heavenly Father who loves me and surrounded me with people who accepted me as part of their families."

Rebecca looked into Elizabeth's eyes. "I have struggled with fear all my life. If I had let my worries continue to paralyze me, I would have missed out on meeting you and your family. You will never know how much I appreciate how welcoming you have been."

Elizabeth brought Rebecca into an embrace. "Oh honey, it has been a pleasure. You are so special to me. I am sorry it took us this long to find each other again. I admit to being apprehensive as well. But, I want to help you make a fresh start with your father. Your mother would have wanted that. She loved him very much."

Sniffing, Elizabeth used a dainty handkerchief to wipe the tears running furiously down her face. "Now look at me I am a watering pot, and as Sara Jane already told you, I am not one of those women who cry prettily. My face gets red, and my nose runs. Most assuredly, if I don't stop, my eyes will be swollen shut."

Laughing, Rebecca embraced Elizabeth. "We can't have that, can we? Sara Jane would be mortified."

Chapter 31

Dear Papa,
Molly asked me to help her with Sam's girls. They are twins and are adorable. B.J. offered to drive me back and forth a couple of days a week so that I can spend more time at the ranch. I am so happy when I am with them. Sam is such a dedicated father, and I admire him so much…

Rebecca enjoyed spending time with Sam as they explored the variety of shops a larger town afforded. They had also taken a drive out to the country to deliver a saddle order to Jonas Weber who took pride in giving them a tour of his ranch.

Later, they all gathered for dinner at the family's country home. Rebecca had been impressed by the beauty of the spacious entry hall and its winding staircase. Sliding doors connected the attractively decorated hall, parlor, library and dining rooms which were octagon in shape. Sam was more impressed by the kitchen's sink pump connected to a cistern which held thousands of gallons of water collected from the slate roof.

After dinner, Hannah excitedly led them past the second floor that housed the bedrooms to the tower, which was a large octagon room the children used as a playroom.

It was a wonderful day. Rebecca felt happy at the opportunity of spending time with good friends. Her enjoyment was so complete, she had almost forgotten her upcoming court date as she chatted happily with Sam about their visit.

They returned to the Brooks' home, and Sara Jane rushed to meet them. "Rebecca, you will never guess, your father came to meet with Mama. He wants to see you."

Wide-eyed Rebecca looked to Sam, whose face contorted into a scowl.

Elizabeth scolded her daughter. "That is quite enough young lady. At least let them get settled before you start carrying on. Why don't you give us a few moments to speak in private?"

Blushing, Sara Jane, apologized profusely. "Oh, I am sorry, I was excited is all."

Elizabeth softened her tone. "Why don't you ask Cook to prepare some coffee? I will let you know when to bring it in, alright?"

Rebecca felt the blood drain from her face as they followed Elizabeth into the parlor to meet with her attorney, Peter Marks. Taking her arm, Sam steered her gently to the settee. "Rebecca, you aren't going to faint on me, are you?"

Not wanting to alarm anyone, she shook her head, sinking into the soft cushions with an outward calmness she did not feel.

Sam took a seat beside Rebecca and squeezed her hand slightly

Peter looked at Rebecca with concern. "Are you sure you are feeling okay? Do you need a little time?"

Rebecca glanced at her hands that were now folded in her lap. "Whatever it is you need to tell me, please, get it over with. I want the truth."

Peter took a seat in a side chair he placed directly in front of her. "After years of your father's head being buried in the sand, he received what one might call an epiphany. Having no one to blame but himself, however—in his defense—the deception regarding your welfare was extreme. The root of the problem is although your father mastered the spoken word, he struggles to read in English. He prefers to do any correspondence in German and delegates any communication or legal documents to those who work for him—and to his wife."

Peter leaned forward. "In theory, his second marriage was a good plan. However, Louisa was not the woman he believed her to be. She has stolen directly from your trust fund for years. Now that your father knows the truth, he wants to make restitution, not only monetarily, but he wants to work to restore your relationship. Or he wishes to meet with you to see if you would be open to working toward that end."

Sam lightly stroked Rebecca's forearm. "What are you thinking? This is good news, isn't it? At least you know your pa wanted to try and take care of you. That counts for something doesn't it?"

Feeling numb to emotion, Rebecca gazed at her hands clasped tightly together in her lap. "I don't know what I expected. I am glad to know at least he wants to meet with me."

"You are thinking he should have tried harder, and a lot earlier, I expect. I couldn't agree with you more. I told your father the same thing and to his face." Rubbing his jaw, Peter continued. "Let me say your father was not at all pleased with my statement. He gave me a small souvenir to reflect his feelings," he said as he used his hand to move his jaw back and forth.

Rebecca's mouth dropped as she noticed a small bruise forming on Peter's jaw. Sam and Peter shared a grin before he turned his attention back to her. "I know your father will want to speak for himself. But he truly believed you were back east getting an education in an environment better for your health. He also was getting updates from the school and the doctors on your progress. He certainly had expenditures indicating you were being cared for at no small cost. In hindsight, we know those communications were lies."

"I can attest to the truth of this statement; your father dedicated himself to making a success of the ranch. He says he did it all for you and in honor of your mother. So many have tried to make a success of things here, but few have succeeded. Your father is the exception to the rule. His hard work will be to your benefit. The bulk of the ranch, the house, the livestock will ultimately be yours. Your father's quest was always to provide for you and his dream was to bring you back to live with him on the ranch one day."

Sam leaned back and cast a worried frown at Peter. "Based on what happened to Rebecca when she was a child, knowing what we know about this stepmother, not to mention her stepsister, how could she ever go back into a situation like that? It would never be safe."

Rebecca tapped her feet impatiently. Surprising herself she interjected, "While I agree it would be foolish to go anywhere near Louisa or Lucy intentionally, I have fond memories of my stepbrother Robby. Since I was a little girl I have dreamed of having a family, and you may think me naïve, but I would like the opportunity to meet my half-brothers."

Peter gave a look of approval to Sam. You are right to be concerned about Louisa and perhaps Lucy also." Rubbing his chin again but with a mischievous smile, he said, "Your father and I had a very productive meeting. I think we understand each other's point of view better now. He did share with me his lawyer is working on a settlement of some sort for Louisa. She and Lucy will be staying in town."

"So, if neither will be at the ranch, do you think I could safely visit my father?"

"Your father is a broken man. I believe he's learned from his mistakes and he would do everything in his power to make sure you are safe. If you take Sam along with you, that is more reason to believe you will be fine."

Elizabeth took this moment to speak. "For added support, my family and I will come along.

We can put Sara Jane as lookout," she said as she reached for Rebecca's hand.

Laughter broke the weightiness of the conversation. Growing serious again, Rebecca turned toward Sam. "You've been here nearly a week already. Would you be able to take some additional time to go and visit my father with me?"

"Adam and I worked it out for me to be able to stay several more days. I would be honored to go with you. If you hadn't asked me, I would have invited myself. But know this, I am going in loaded for bear. If someone so much as looks at you funny, they will hear about it from me."

Chuckling, Peter slapped Sam on the back saying, "You are a good man, Sam Brady. In many ways, I agree it will be best to be prepared. However, I truly believe the worst is over. The hard part will be to forgive and move on."

Elizabeth cleared her throat. "Peter, why don't you and I give these two a moment to talk? Y'all join us in the dining room when you are ready. I know Sara Jane will be anxious to get your reactions to things."

As Peter and Elizabeth exited, Sam turned to Rebecca. "This is what you want, to go and see your Pa face to face?"

"For years I have wanted to meet with him, to talk with him. But now I don't know—I am feeling anxious and a little scared."

"I admit to feeling a little uneasy myself. Not only am I worried about how you are feeling, but also what it is going to take to keep you safe. From the sound of things, you are going to be somewhat well to do. Which leads me to the question, if that is true, what will you want with someone like me?"

Shaking her head, Rebecca bit her lip before replying. "Sam, do you remember earlier this year how you would get so frustrated with me every time I spoke to you about a concern? No matter what or how I said it, you supposed I was trying to pressure you into marrying me?"

Sam took in a deep breath and took Rebecca's hand. "Going forward please know I will do my best never to treat you that way again. I want you to tell me when something is worrying you."

Rebecca stared at Sam's hand now holding hers and sighed. "If we were to get married, we would vow to love each other in sickness and in health for richer and for poorer. Should this inheritance be valid, we might be richer than we could have imagined, but I don't think richer makes anyone necessarily happier. We have both seen evidence of that. I imagine having extensive property brings about other problems."

Rebecca squeezed Sam's hand and looked into his eyes before continuing. "Since you came to visit me here, I have been so happy. When I wake up each day, I feel the need to pinch myself to make sure I am not dreaming. But I also worry I might say or do something which will make you leave. It seems strange to me that you ask, why would I want someone like you when I wonder what you want with someone like me?"

Shaking his head in disbelief, Sam said, "I guess that makes us quite the pair, doesn't it?" Taking both hands, he continued. "Rebecca Leah Towns

Mueller, I love you. I am sorry if my actions caused you to believe otherwise. I don't want another day to go by without you knowing how much I want you to be my wife and a mother to my girls. I want to spend the rest of my life making you happy, showing you how much you mean to me."

"I want to do this again." Sam knelt beside her on one knee. "Would you do me the honor of marrying me? Would you commit to loving this mostly poorer but crazy in love with you cowboy?"

"Most definitely," Rebecca said with a grin.

At that, Sam stood, kissed her soundly, and spun her around in his arms.

Grabbing tightly to his shoulders, Rebecca cried out, "Sam, no. Don't spin me."

Stopping immediately and setting her down, Sam groaned. "I can't believe I just did that."

Clutching his shoulders, looking at her feet trying to steady herself, Rebecca replied, "We went from better to worse, real quick, didn't we?"

Chapter 32

Dear Papa,
Mr. Marks retired, and Peter has taken over the business. I don't know why, but his new wife took me in dislike. She asked me to make myself scarce. Mrs. Potts offered me a job at her diner. I will start working there next week...

Still seething from the most recent conversation with his wife, Charles gathered his sons and walked with them to the mercantile. The shop owner patiently pulled objects from the display case. Charles patted both boys on the shoulder, then pointed towards the merchandise. "Your mother says we must pick from these preselected items. Take a moment to decide what you would like to give your sister for her birthday and going away present. You must hurry. I have an appointment. I don't want to be late."

Charles glanced at his timepiece. His much-anticipated meeting with his daughter Becky and his lawyer was this morning. How he would ever make things up to her, he couldn't begin to fathom. For a moment he allowed himself to be distracted. He watched his sons shop for their sister, Lucy.

Mark scowled at the selection the salesperson painstakingly laid out on red velvet fabric. "Can't imagine wanting any of this for my birthday. You pick, Charlie."

Looking at the assortment of items he agreed with his youngest son's assessment. What his stepdaughter would need with another fan or lace handkerchief he would never know. Charlie turned toward the selection of barrettes and hat pins and placed his finger on his mouth. Mark fidgeted pulling on his father's sleeve. "Pa, is it okay if I go look at the fishing poles in the back of the store?"

Charles sighed. "Mark, understand we are not here to shop for you. However, you may go for a minute or two only. Come directly back. I will need to leave soon."

~

Rebecca rejected another pair of shoes and placed them back on the shelf. *I can't believe these prices.* She smiled at a young boy of about six or seven who watched her from behind a display of fishing poles. Upon meeting his gaze, the boy gasped, turned and ran directly into Sam.

Sam steadied the boy. "Well hello there, partner, everything okay?"

The boy's eyes widened. He pointed at Rebecca. "Mister, is she an angel?"

Sam laughed and pushed his hat back from his face and replied, "Well I admit she is mighty pretty, sweet too. But an angel? No, she's flesh and bone, the same as you and me, kid."

Curious, Rebecca did not attempt to move closer but watched Sam's interaction with the child from a distance. When the boy caught her eye, he shivered, then ran toward the front of the store.

Sam scratched his head as he approached her. "The strangest thing just happened. The kid that just ran into me wanted to know if you were an angel."

Rebecca laughed. "Well, I know you set him straight."

"I tried, but I think you spooked him. If you are going to get a pair of shoes, you best pick so you will have time to try them on. We will need to start making our way over to the law office soon."

Rebecca waved her hand in dismissal. "I think I am going to have to pass. The prices are higher here than in Carrie Town."

Rebecca took Sam's arm. I noticed the little fellow watching me, but when I acknowledged him, he took off and ran straight into you."

As they approached the front of the store, Sam put his finger against his mouth and motioned with his head towards the young child who dragged an older but reluctant boy towards them. The younger spoke. "You've got to come with me. It's her."

"What are you talking about, Mark? Who is her?"

The younger boy Rebecca heard referred to by the name Mark grabbed the older boy's arm and pulled. "The lady in Pa's watch. See for yourself. Hurry before she gets away."

The boys turned the corner and stopped directly

in front of Rebecca and Sam.

Sam nodded at the young boy. "Hello again, I see you brought reinforcements."

Sam placed his hand on Rebecca's arm. "This is the young man I told you about. Your latest admirer I believe," he said with a wink.

Rebecca knelt in front of the boy. His curly brown hair, brown eyes, and a spattering of freckles across his nose painted an adorable picture. "Hello, my name is Rebecca, it's very nice to meet you."

A shadow loomed above, and Rebecca craned her neck looking into a startling familiar face. Her eyes locked on the man even as she watched his large hands come down gently on the boy's shoulders. They were the same hands that long ago had thrown her into the air safely, catching her as she squealed with delight. "Do it again Papa." Hands that comforted her, held and made her feel safe.

Rebecca broke into a cold sweat. Another memory came to mind. Suddenly she felt five years old again, as she observed the giant of a man whose face wore a familiar frown.

"Boys, did you not hear me calling? Come, we must go. I have an appointment. My apologies, ma'am." With a tip of his hat, he turned his sons around to head towards the door. *He doesn't recognize me.* Rebecca stood slowly. She watched the young boy tug on her father's sleeve.

"But Pa, it's the lady."

Charles Mueller ruffled the boy's hair. "Come now. I told you I am in a hurry."

The boy's mouth formed into a pout. He pulled

on her father's arm more forcefully. "Pa, please wait, it's *your* lady."

Her father seemed unaffected by the remark. He placed one hand on each boy and steered them towards the front of the store. Frowning, he stopped mid-step. "My lady?"

Rebecca watched the older boy roll his eyes in her direction. She felt her breath catch. "Pa, Mark thinks she is the woman in the picture. The one in your pocket watch."

Charles slowly looked from his son and turned towards Rebecca. For a moment time stood still. She'd dreamed of a reunion with her father since she was a little girl. He would be overjoyed to see her, open his arms and welcome her in a warm embrace. All would be well.

The lines around her father's eyes softened. The shock she felt sure must be reflected in her own seemed to melt into another emotion, one that brought sudden moisture to her father's eyes. "Becky?"

Blue eyes flecked with green, so like her own, met hers. "Hello, Papa."

Still frowning, his voice rough, he said, "Forgive me for not recognizing you." He shook his head. "You seem well."

I suppose we are to converse like polite strangers. Rebecca lifted her chin. "Yes, your boots are quite safe, at least for the time being."

Her father pinched the bridge of his nose. His mouth opened and closed but he didn't speak.

Rebecca's hand trembled as she tucked a stray lock of hair behind her ear. She was relieved to feel

Sam place her arm in his. He tilted his head towards the other customers in the mercantile. "I believe it best if we go somewhere less public to speak."

Charles glowered, his body rigid. "What business is this of yours?"

Rebecca's eyes widened. For a brief moment, she watched both men stand still and assess each other.

Sam sidestepped and maneuvered around her father without missing a beat. "We will see you shortly at the attorney's office."

Chapter 33

Dear Papa,
I didn't think I would enjoy working at the diner but find I am content. The work keeps me busy, and I enjoy hearing the conversations between the customers. They discuss everything from the price of cattle to crossbreeding...

After leaving the mercantile, Sam suggested they stop at the local diner. "Let's take a break here and get some coffee. That will give us a little time to get our wits about us."

Rebecca wiped her tears and forced herself to relax in the cheerful atmosphere. She admired the large window that showered the room with sunshine, highlighting red gingham oilcloths on the tables. After being coaxed by Sam, she took a bite of the piece of apple pie he ordered. "I don't usually like to eat sweets so early in the day. Still, this is delicious." Closing her eyes, she took another bite, savoring the flavor.

"Your Pa called you Becky. I don't recall anyone else using the nickname."

Rebecca shook her head. "He is the only one who ever did. But he had all sorts of nicknames for me from what I recall. Liebling is another name he used a lot."

Sam reached for Rebecca's hand and gave it a light squeeze. "Liebling?"

She took another bite of pie. "It's a German word for sweetheart."

Rebecca looked out the window and sighed. "No matter how often I thought of a reunion with my father, I would never have imagined what just happened. I thought he would be glad to see me. Somehow, I would know he loved me. The way he glared, I felt like I a little girl again and in big trouble."

"Try to give it a little more time, honey. Though, I admit just the size of your Pa is intimidating. You are such a tiny little thing. I pictured your Pa as small too. Sure, didn't imagine he'd be akin to a grizzly bear. Though I've got to say, the way you described his shoes doesn't do them justice. Those are the fanciest boots, I ever saw."

Sam's eyebrows rose as Rebecca took the last bite of pie. "I sure am glad you aren't one to eat sweets early in the day. Otherwise, I would have to order the whole pie," he added with a wide grin.

Rebecca gasped. "Sam, I don't know what has gotten into me. I am sorry."

Sam chuckled. "Not a problem. I just have never seen you eat something with so much enthusiasm."

Rebecca continued circling her spoon in vain, on the empty plate. "I suppose those were my brothers. This situation doesn't seem real, and yet I feel anxious."

Sam squeezed Rebecca's hand. "The smaller boy, the one they called Mark, he seemed inclined to agree about the anxious part. You made him nervous."

Rebecca placed the spoon down and sighed. "This whole thing is more taxing than I anticipated."

Sam eyed his now empty plate. "We still have a little time to kill. I will order us another piece of pie. Or should I make it two?"

Rebecca stared out the window. "Nothing for me, thanks. I don't eat sweets this early in the day."

Chapter 33

Dear Papa,
I think I may be in love with Adam's brother Sam. He is wonderful…

Placing his hands on his sons' shoulders, Charles hurried them towards home. Lost in his thoughts, he silenced the peppering of questions with a growl. "Enough." Both boys rushed to keep pace with the long strides of their father but remained quiet.

Arriving at the door, Charles kneeled at eye level with his sons. "Charlie, Mark, forgive me for losing my temper. None of this is your fault. Later, we will sit and discuss this fully. In the meantime, I must leave to make my appointment."

Mark rubbed his nose and sniffled.

Charles reached in his pocket and handed his handkerchief to his youngest son. "All right, one question, what is bothering you?"

Mark's bottom lip trembled. "Pa, the angel, does

she want to take you with her?"

Charles frowned. "Angel?"

Charlie pointed his thumb towards his brother. "Pa, he thinks the lady at the mercantile is the woman whose picture you carry in your pocket watch."

Charles opened his timepiece and blinked rapidly. "Boys, the young lady is indeed in this tintype." Pointing at the picture, he explained. "The little girl is my daughter, your sister, who is now quite grown up. I am going to speak with her this morning. It is my hope one day soon, to be able to bring her to meet you both."

Mark's jaw dropped. "But Pa, she shouldn't be here. Mama told us your daughter is…" He looked at Charlie and asked, "What does she call it?"

"Disturbed and not fit for polite society," Charlie answered stoically.

Taking a deep breath, Charles kept his voice even, "Nonsense. You saw her. She is quite well. You will forget whatever your mother told you about your sister. Do you understand?"

Mark drew circles with his boots. "But Pa, we already got one sister. Ain't that enough?" Surprising himself, Charles laughed. Not a soft chuckle, but a full belly laugh.

Looking at the astonished expressions on his sons' faces, he replied. "Nonetheless you have two sisters. Now go into the house. The housekeeper will be waiting for you."

Chapter 34

Dear Papa,
My friend Lois inherited some money and used it to open her own dress shop. I think she is very courageous. Her father thinks she is foolish. He told her not to come running home when the shop fails. I am worried about her.

Rebecca's attorney, Peter Marks studied the documents outlining the expenditures from Rebecca's inheritance. "According to the stipulations of the will, the house, land, and a percentage of the livestock will one day belong to you. Based on the amount embezzled from the estate, even if your father sold everything not tied to your inheritance, it would be less than you are owed."

Peter took a chair and seated himself across from Rebecca and Sam. "Your stepmother not only utilized your funds for her excessive spending habits but found a way to allot money for both your stepsiblings' education. Knowing your kind heart, I hope you won't decide to forgive all and forget."

Rebecca traced the scar on her palm, absently. "Papa Horace and Eloise sacrificed so much for me. All the while Lucy and my stepmother robbed them of money due, and me of both home and father."

Sam gave Rebecca's hand a light squeeze. "I notice you mentioned Lucy. Don't forget your stepbrother received a college education at your expense, also."

Rebecca turned towards Sam. "What do you think I should do?"

Sam cleared his throat. "This needs to be your decision. However, I will say this. When people take advantage of a defenseless child, it seems appropriate they feel some discomfort and be made to make things right."

Rebecca straightened and raised her chin. "My stepbrother, Robby, was kind to me. Honestly, I don't believe I would be here if he hadn't brought help for me the day I was locked in my room. Rebecca bit her lip. "Because of what he did for me, I would like to forgive the expenses related to his education."

Sam shook his head slowly. "Do you feel inclined to forgive the costs for your stepsister's schooling?"

Rebecca felt her cheeks burn. "I don't feel anything of the sort. In fact, I would request the full amount be paid first, along with any interest which would have accrued."

Not understanding the look, she saw on Sam's face, Rebecca asked, "You think I am terrible, don't you?"

"Not at all, honey. I am just surprised you could decide quickly and with such feeling, so sure of your choice."

"I do feel good about it." Rebecca picked up a pad and pencil. "Next, I would like to discuss a plan on how to reimburse Papa Horace's estate, which now belongs to Adam and Sam. Elizabeth told me my father owns a small herd of Herefords he is raising for purebred stock."

Rebecca tapped her mouth with a pencil. "Sam, selecting livestock as compensation, could provide you and Adam with some new bulls for crossbreeding a little sooner than originally planned. Although I think it should be stipulated, the choices would be hand selected. Should you agree to it, an agreement like this could benefit my father also if he is cash-strapped. What do you think?"

Sam whistled. "A good Hereford bull is pricey."

Peter popped the financial ledger with the back of his hand and laughed. "If I didn't know better I would swear Horace is in this room giving you advice, Rebecca. But based on the amount owed, it seems you could get more than one prize bull and some additional cattle to boot. That could go a long way in revitalizing the ranch."

Rebecca smiled at the reference to her guardian, also Sam's uncle. She recalled his support for her thirst for knowledge with fondness. With every new achievement, Rebecca couldn't wait to tell Horace and inevitably he would encourage her to write her father. His encouragement knew no bounds. *I wonder would he agree with my plan?*

Sam smiled then nodded at Rebecca. "I would want to talk things over with Adam. But I can't imagine he would be anything less than thrilled. If things pan out, the idea of starting a small purebred stock sounds like a mighty good idea. Applying what Horace taught us about diversifying, we could also put one bull out on our open range for crossbreeding."

Peter chuckled. "I believe Horace taught you both well. Of course, we could request a certain amount of cash also. While y'all are meeting with Rebecca's father, I will be in conference with his attorney to outline this offer in principle. Are you still agreeable to the meeting?"

Chapter 35

Dear Papa,
Uncle Horace used the expression from time to time that he was so mad he could spit. I never really understood his feelings until now. I don't know how it is possible to love someone and still be so angry with them at the same time. Molly says it is normal…

Charles entered his attorney's office with a clenched jaw. "I have seen my daughter, Jacob. She looks surprisingly healthy, although the state of her shoes suggests she lives in poverty."

Jacob moved to close the door to his office. "You must remember, she lived on her own for years. It must have been difficult for her to make ends meet."

Charles wiped his hand through his hair. "I find it hard to believe Horace would not have provided for her, especially when I did not."

"Like many in the area, during the last blizzard

before his death, Horace's ranch got walloped. By the time his nephews inherited, things were in dire straits. My guess is, there was nothing financial left."

Charles dropped his head. "My daughter, I know so little about her."

Scowling, he began to pace. "I saw her with some cowboy. Do you know who he is?"

"I imagine he is her intended, Horace's youngest nephew, Sam Brady." Jacob rose from his chair and set on the edge of his desk.

"Out of the question. She is too young to marry."

"She is of age to do as she wishes." Jacob pulled on his collar. "Be that as it may, my sources say he is a good sort, honest, dependable, excellent father."

"Father?" Charles waved his large hand in the air. "I do not want my daughter saddled with another man's children."

"It seems Becky has made her choice. My suggestion is to take it slow. Take time to know her, before you start trying to run off her beau."

"With my sons, I can teach them to rope, ride, build a campfire." Charles placed his hands on his hips. "What does one do with a daughter?"

Jacob Weber placed his palm beneath his chin, and his fingers tapped his mouth. "My girls like to shop."

Groaning, Charles took a seat before he covered his face with his hands.

~

Rebecca's attorney, Peter Marks inclined his head towards the open door. "I will be conferring with your father's lawyer separately. We thought you might want some privacy. Mr. Weber offered his office for your use. Is that acceptable?"

Rebecca clinched her hands together and nodded.

Sam winked, then placed Rebecca's hand in the crook of his arm. As they entered the prestigious law office, a sweet aroma of cherry wood pipe tobacco filled the air. Rebecca blinked as her eyes became accustomed to the dark-paneled walls.

Her father rose to his full height of six feet four inches, wearing a familiar scowl. "Hello, Becky."

Rebecca paused and took in a deep breath. "Good morning again, Papa."

Charles' eyes narrowed at Sam. He motioned towards a pair of chairs. "Please take a seat."

Rebecca felt Sam's arm guide her to an armchair. She blinked rapidly. *I will not cry in front of this man.* "Papa, I would like you to meet, Sam Brady, my fiancé. Sam this is my father, Charles Mueller.

Charles glared at Sam. His hands opened and closed in fists in rapid succession. "Since just meeting after all these years, am I to lose you again so quickly?"

Sam extended his hand in greeting. "The decision to pursue a relationship is going to depend on your actions, Mr. Mueller."

Their hands locked briefly in a standoff. Both men stared at one another. Charles released his grip, but his jaw remained clenched. "What gives you the right to speak of such things?"

Rebecca stared at the two men. Although Sam

possessed broad shoulders and a muscular stature, he seemed small as he stood next to her father.

"Rebecca has done me the honor of agreeing to be my wife," Sam said. "I am here to support her and ensure her safety."

"Safety? I would not hurt my daughter."

Sam met his glare. "Based on your history, I reckon that remains to be seen."

Charles' face grew red. He pinched the bridge of his nose. "From what you know of me, you are right to question my sincerity."

Rubbing his hand through his hair, her father crossed the room and sat in a chair opposite Rebecca. His voice cracked. "Please know I love you and it has been my driving force to fulfill the plans your mother and I had for you. The house, the ranch, the cattle, everything is part of our dream, and I swore to your mother on her deathbed I would make it a reality."

Charles reached for Rebecca's hand then seemed to think better of it. "I should not have married so quickly after your mother's death. But I was lonely and believed you needed a mother. I thought Lucy would be a bonus." He forced a laugh. "I assumed she would be a wonderful playmate for you."

Her father looked away for a moment and rubbed the back of his neck. "Although your stepmother devised the deception, this is my fault. I should have been in contact, seen for myself you were provided for. Frankly, it was easier to throw myself into my work, my new family. I am ashamed of myself."

Rebecca flinched. Her father's admission although not surprising, was painful. "Why did you reject my letters?"

Charles' face flushed red. "I've been deceived about so many things—your health, your education, even where you lived. I had no idea the letters existed until recently." He cleared his throat. "After the injury to your hand and subsequently your fever and bouts with pneumonia, it was vital that you be in the care of a better doctor and someone who could dedicate the attention necessary to help you to get well."

Rebecca fought the urge not to pull back as her father took her hand. Their eyes met, his now misty. "I hoped that you would regain your strength and be able to return home. "

"I spent more time away from the ranch than at home. It was clear to me that your stepmother was not capable of providing you with the type of assistance required."

Rebecca's eyes shifted to the path of a solitary tear slowly moving along her father's cheek. Horace and Eloise loved you, and you loved them. They dedicated themselves to doing whatever was necessary to help you regain your health."

Her father looked down at her hand and gave it a light squeeze. ."When it became clear that your road to recovery was going to be a long one, I allowed others to tell me, what was in your best interest. My contact with you would be limited to allow for a more natural transition. My involvement would be financial, but I would receive updates on your progress. I did indeed receive updates. Until recently, I believed you were back east, in a climate that was better for your condition."

Rebecca swallowed hard then lifted her chin, waiting for him to continue.

"Liebling, I have been a fool." Her father leaned forward. "You have every right to deny me. But I would like to beg your forgiveness. Starting today, I want to do everything in my power to at least try and forge a relationship. Please give me a chance."

Rebecca forced herself to breathe evenly. She looked at Sam who offered her a nod of encouragement. For a moment she said nothing. Memories of a conversation, years ago about her father's absence came to mind. *I don't care what the reason might be. If he were to show up tomorrow to see me, I would be so happy.*

Summoning her courage, she smiled. "What do you have in mind?"

Charles stared at his daughter as he blew out a sigh of apparent relief. His face relaxed, and his mouth turned upwards slightly. "I would like to spend time with you, get to know you and your beau."

Her father glanced at Sam and frowned again. Rebecca felt Sam stiffen.

Rebecca took in a slow deep breath. She watched her father draw out his handkerchief and mop his face. Turning towards Sam, he apologized. "It is difficult for me to believe my daughter is old enough to have a beau. In my mind, she is still a little girl. Please accept my apology and allow me to show you around town. I would like to introduce you to some of my friends, and we can do some shopping."

"Shopping?" Rebecca's eyebrows rose.

"You like to shop, do you not?"

Rebecca met her father's gaze. "I've never had much need for shopping."

Charles' mouth dropped. "Since when is need a requirement for a woman to shop?"

Rebecca studied her father. "What other reason would there be?"

Charles slapped his legs with mirth. "Tell me, Becky, what do you enjoy?"

Rebecca lifted her chin and answered. "I like to read and bake, and I love working with numbers."

Charles smiled. "Growing up with Horace, I should not be surprised you like to read and enjoy working with numbers. But I thought all women liked to shop."

Sam interjected. "Mr. Mueller, if you dislike shopping as I do, you might be pleased to know Rebecca also enjoys fishing."

Rebecca beamed at Sam, before turning towards her father. "I do love to fish. But I have to avoid the heat, so early in the morning is best."

Charles opened and closed his hands and once again glared at Sam.

Rebecca took in a deep breath. *Every time Sam says something it seems to make my father angry.*

"Fishing will have to wait for another day." Charles motioned towards Rebecca's shoes. "I believe there is an obvious need that could be eliminated by a shopping trip. It is past time for a new pair of boots, don't you agree?"

Rebecca felt her cheeks flame. She looked at the floor taking in the image of her worn out boots.

Charles cleared his throat. "I happen to know an excellent bootmaker. What do you say, you and your beau accompany me to his shop? Offering a half smile, he continued. "Afterwards I would like to take you both to dinner. There is a diner close by. They make an excellent apple pie."

Chapter 36

Dear Papa,
Prices in town are sky high. I can no longer afford to take meals at the boarding house. Mrs. Potts is wonderful. She makes sure I eat something before I start my shift.

Rebecca and Sam strolled towards the bootmaker's shop and listened to her father's explanation of how he had become acquainted with the cobbler.

Charles' face lit with enthusiasm. "I purchased my first pair of boots in this style in Kansas. Several years ago, I bought this building and convinced the same cobbler to move here and set up business. We now employ six other shoemakers who do repair work but primarily make custom boots."

Rebecca felt her face flush. She looked down and wiggled her toes. She felt the familiar hole in the sole of her shoe. *I have newspaper lining my boots, and my father owns a shoe store.* "You own this shop?"

Charles waved his hand towards the two-story stone building. "I own the structure, but Ralph and I are partners. He is a very talented bootmaker. Come in, and I will introduce you."

Rebecca took in the scene of the busy shop. Several cobblers sat on benches working. The walls were filled with forms used to make and repair customers' footwear, and rows of boot samples.

Charles extended his hand to a cobbler. "Ralph, there is someone here I want you to meet. This is my daughter, Becky and her intended, Sam Brady."

The cobbler placed his hammer on the workbench and removed nails from his mouth. Shaking Sam's hand, he turned and smiled broadly at Rebecca. "Becky, it is wonderful to meet you. You are a vision, so like your mother."

Rebecca placed her hand over her heart and smiled. "You knew my mother?"

The cobbler's smile drooped, and he shook his head. "No. Not personally, but your papa here has shown me her picture many times. He carried it with him for as long as I have known him."

Charles patted the man on his back roughly. "Ralph, I need for you to create something special for my daughter and my future son-in-law. Nothing but the best will do."

Beaming, Charles took a sample pair of black riding boots with no lacing and a pointed toe and handed them to Sam. "What do you think about these?" Charles pointed at the intricate design of the leather and the bright yellow stitching. "If you like, Ralph can add more color or design. Anything you want."

Sam's jaw dropped, and he stammered. "No, Mr. Mueller, I couldn't accept a gift like that. The boots I have still have plenty of wear in them. On the other hand, Rebecca's boots are way past needing to be replaced."

Charles waved his hand in the air. "Nonsense. Allow me the pleasure to do something for you both."

Turning back to the wall, he picked up an ornate pair of ladies' boots and turned toward Rebecca. "Now then daughter, come and pick out something for yourself. The ladies all seem to want buttons and laces. What do you say?"

Rebecca suppressed a giggle. *Those are the most impractical boots I have ever seen.* "Well, I have never given it much thought. I suppose I try to buy something reasonably priced and that can hold up to a lot of wear and tear. The pair you are holding doesn't seem to fit in either of those categories."

Charles stroked his chin then turned back towards Rebecca. "There are many choices here. Why don't you show me what you like?"

Rebecca looked at several of the more serviceable boots and shook her head at a price. *I thought the prices in the mercantile were high.*

Rebecca's father frowned, shook his head, then turned the price tag over. "Forget the money. Find something you like, my treat."

Rebecca felt her face flame when her father's partner insisted he help to remove her boots. Only this morning, Sam had offered again to purchase her a new pair. "Rebecca, how those boots have remained in one piece is a testament that miracles still happen. One might even say you are a walking miracle," he'd joked. She declined because of the expense. *I can't believe I am about to become the owner of custom footwear designed specifically for me.*

Rebecca pondered over a variety of styles then looked at her father's hopeful face. "Come now, Liebling. Those boots you have chosen are certainly serviceable, but they are so plain."

Charles held out a sample pair of lace-up pointy-toed boots. The white leather foot of the boot met with a massive black decorative star with silver stitching. "What do you think of these?"

Rebecca stared, then placed her hand over her mouth trying to suppress her horror. *I think he must like the style. One thing is for sure, if anyone saw me wearing them, they would believe fancy boots must be a family trait.* Not meeting her father's eyes, she stammered. "Those are very nice."

Charles smiled happily. "Now we are getting somewhere. Go ahead and pick a pair of ready-made boots and I will have Ralph design you something special."

Taking the boot with him, he walked towards the back of the shop. "Ralph, my daughter finally made a selection."

Rebecca met Sam's gaze, and they laughed softly together.

Sam whispered. "Since I don't generally tuck my pants in my boots, no one will ever see the decorative stitching. Fancy footwear is something a man of my status might never be able to pull off. I can hear the ranch hands now. But your pa as big and foreboding as he is, no one would dare say a thing to him. Not to mention they are mighty fine boots."

Rebecca giggled. "No one will be able to see the design on mine either since my skirts will cover all but the tops of the boots."

Sam nodded his head towards Rebecca's father. "While I appreciate the fact we both will have a new pair of shoes, your father seems to be gaining the most satisfaction."

Chapter 37

Three Months Later in Carrie Town

Dear Papa,
I know now what it means when people say love makes you do funny things…

Sam searched for Rebecca's wedding ring in vain before he remembered yesterday's conversation with Adam. "You are strung tighter than a barbed wire fence. Leave the ring with me. I will pin it to your best man's pocket," he said with a wink and a slap to Seth's shoulder. "Emma's got the wedding clothes ready. But she said to remind you to fix the girls' hair."

He peered out the window at Sadie and Grace. Thankfully their hair remained in papers. The girls were making the most of the beautiful day, dressed in overalls playing with a chicken. He'd spent more than an hour preparing their hair last night. He blew out a breath of relief. It had been a long time since he rolled the girls hair on his own, but Molly was busy with her new babies, and Emma was spending the night in town with Rebecca in preparation for the wedding.

He walked outside, took in a deep breath of the crisp autumn air and blew out slowly. *Why in the world do they insist on playing with an animal I would otherwise designate for dinner?* "Girls leave the hen alone. Come in here and get dressed."

Sadie stood and placed one hand on her hip. "Pa, Aunt Molly said we have to stay like this until the very last minute. Is it almost time to go?"

Sam forced a smile. "No honey, you are right. We've still got plenty of time. I am just antsy, I guess." Sam walked closer to his twins.

"I guess getting married does that to a person," Grace said as she put down the animal, which made a loud squawking sound in protest. She took one of Sam's hands and patted it.

Sadie pulled on Sam's other hand. "Wait til you see what Petunia can do. Grandpa says she is the smartest chicken he ever met."

Sam's eyebrows rose. "Grandpa?"

Grace narrowed her eyes and studied him stoically. "You know, Rebecca's father. He told us to call him, Grandpa."

Sam felt his jaw drop. Recovering quickly, he nodded at both girls. *The man can barely tolerate being in the same room with me, and he wants my kids to call him Grandpa?* "Well, that is mighty nice of Grandpa."

Sadie placed her hands back on her hips. "Pa,

only me and Grace can call him by that name."

Grace leaned forward and spoke softly. "It's probably best if you keep calling him Mr. Mueller."

Sam coughed to subdue his laughter. "That sounds like mighty fine advice." Unable to fully contain his mirth, he grinned. "Alright now, girls, what did you want to show me? Have you taught Petunia a new trick?"

Sadie crossed her arms across her chest. "We didn't have to teach her she just does it. Watch." Sadie bent down and clapped her hands. "Come here, Petunia."

Sam watched the hen scratch and dig in the dirt, lift her head and become almost rigid in her stance. She paused then sprinted towards Sadie and Grace, with a loud squawk and flapping wings.

Grace opened her arms wide. "Here, Petunia."

For the second time in just a few minutes, his jaw dropped. His would be Sunday dinner snuggled into his daughter's embrace.

"Why she ran faster than a hot knife slices through butter." Sam stepped closer noting how the hen curled her head into his daughter's neck. "Well, don't that beat all. She looks like she is hugging you back."

"She's cuddling, Pa." Sadie grinned, displaying several missing teeth. "Rebecca says Miss Lois gives the best hugs. But I expect the reason is because she ain't ever hugged Petunia. We can't wait to show her, can we Gracie?"

Grace nodded in agreement as she smoothed the bird's feathers, softly crooning.

Sam rubbed his chin. "Girls, I know you love

Petunia, but I am just not so sure playing with a chicken is well…clean."

"Do you want us to give her a bath, Pa?" Grace asked.

Sam held his hands up in surrender. "No, don't go getting any ideas. Whatever you do, you are not to try to bathe that chicken."

Sam took in his daughters' earnest expressions and pushed his hat to the back of his head. "I tell you what, why don't we go check on Mama dog and see how her puppies are doing? In just another week or so those pups should be ready to be weaned. Now you talk about a good pet. There is a reason why people say dogs are man's best friend."

Sadie put her finger to her chin. "What do they say about chickens?"

"Well, you ask a good question." Sam looked at the chicken which seemed to mimic his daughter's inquisitive stare. *If I didn't know better, I would say she is listening to see how I am going to answer.* Sam snapped his fingers. "I've got one. Whistling women and crowing hens always come to no good end."

Grace placed her hand over her mouth and gasped. "Pa, that's not funny."

"Besides Emma whistles all the time," Sadie added.

Sam rubbed his chin. "True, and in my mind, there is nothing wrong with a woman whistling, but as far as crowing hens…"

"Pa," both girls cried.

Sam waved his hand. "Oh, don't get your feathers ruffled."

The girls joined him in laughter and skipped to the barn.

Sam stopped when he noticed the chicken followed. "Girls, does Petunia follow you everywhere you go?"

Grace and Sadie nodded in unison.

Sam stood still. Petunia cocked her head and scratched the dirt. "I am not sure how Mama dog will feel about her visiting the puppies. Time will tell. After we have a look, it will be about time for us to get ready for the wedding."

Sam cringed as the girls let loose high-pitched squeals of delight which caused additional squawks and flapping wings from Petunia.

Grace twirled happily in a circle. "Grandpa said he is coming in a carriage to pick us up, so we won't get dusty riding to church."

Sadie held a long lock of hair wrapped up in paper for review. "Aunt Molly said to be careful when you brush our hair, so you don't pull the curl out."

Sam tapped the tip of Sadie's nose. "Since I wrapped each one of those curls, I believe I should be trusted not to undo all my hard work, don't you?"

Sadie nodded while Grace added, "You do exceptional work, Pa."

Pulling both girls into an embrace, he kissed the tops of their heads. "Let's check on those puppies. Afterward, you girls need to wash up and change. Then I will carefully comb those curls."

Grace wagged her finger. "You too, Pa. Don't forget to shave."

Sam rubbed his hand across his chin and grinned sheepishly. "Sure am glad you girls are here to keep me straight. I will do my best to make myself presentable. I don't want to give Rebecca any reason not to agree when Pastor Nelson asks her if she wants to marry me."

Sadie and Grace faced each other, smiled and said. "We don't either Pa."

Hope Final

Chapter 38

Dear Papa,
Sam asked me to be his wife. I said yes….

The blue silk skirt moved freely as Rebecca twirled in front of the full-length mirror. Her mother's wedding gown fit perfectly. "I am glad we decided to forgo the hoop skirt." She ran her hand and felt the smoothness of the silk. The design was a double-layered, draped overskirt in baby blue. "Lois, the floral pattern on the jacket matches perfectly. The lace details and stand collar you added make the whole ensemble look identical to the one from your fashion magazines."

Rebecca pressed one hand to her stomach while Lois circled her again with a critical eye. "You needed a jacket to accommodate for the cooler weather." Lois placed her finger to her mouth, paused then smiled. "Your dress contains the something old, new, and blue."

Rebecca sighed. "Goodness, I didn't realize I was holding my breath. You had me worried for a moment."

Emma unfolded Rebecca's grandmother's handmade veil. "Nonsense, you look lovely." A tear rolled down Rebecca's cheek as she bent her head to allow Emma to place the Brussels lace over her head. *I can't believe this day is finally here.*

Lois took the headpiece she fashioned with wax flowers and placed it over the veil. "Perfect. You are a vision."

Blinking back tears, Molly handed her a lace handkerchief. "I carried this in my wedding. I hoped you would use it for your something borrowed."

Rebecca took in a deep breath, blinked rapidly and offered a watery smile. "I can't thank you all enough. I am blessed." She reached to embrace the three women and laughed when she felt the familiar pat on her back from Lois.

Elizabeth walked into the room carrying a package. "What's this? You ladies know better than to give in to tears. You'll spoil your looks. You best cut out the crying, or I am going to get Sara Jane."

"Don't you dare," Emma sniffed. "There are too many women in here as it is."

Elizabeth waved her hand. "Not at all. Besides I come bearing gifts." She placed the package on the table. "Your father sent this, along with a penny. I assume they are wedding shoes. Do you want me to unwrap the parcel?"

Rebecca felt her stomach lurch. She looked at

her satin slippers. *I don't even want to think about what he might have selected.* "Frankly, I am afraid to look."

Elizabeth unwrapped the package. "Don't be silly. I am sure your father's taste is very ..."

Rebecca looked into the shocked faces of the women she held dear. *Now I know what people mean by the silence was deafening.* Molly stared. Lois looked away. Elizabeth held one dainty, gloved hand over her mouth, and Emma was crying. No, she was laughing. Not able to withhold her curiosity Rebecca hurried over to see the most outlandish pair of boots she'd ever laid eyes on.

Molly recovered first. "Rebecca, I feel certain your father meant well." She picked up one boot and ran her hand over the leather. "I am sure they will be comfortable and more practical than slippers, especially for a wedding this late in the fall."

Lois reached for the other boot. "Since I've more time to look, I believe they will be fine. Your dress will cover all but the foot of the boot. You won't see the design at all."

Emma put an arm around Rebecca. "I am sorry for laughing. But when Elizabeth unwrapped the package, I remembered what you told me about you and your father's shopping trip. You mentioned he loved ornate patterns. He wanted to surprise you."

Rebecca studied the pointy-toed pull-on boots, made of a hand-tooled dark brown leather. The tips of the shoe were plain until exploding into a design of colorful flowers with decorative stitching above the base of the boot.

Rebecca swallowed. "The design is not something I would pick for myself. But the more I think of the effort he must have gone to. I really am touched."

Lois pointed at Rebecca's headpiece. "Orange blossoms, the design on your boots are Orange blossoms. I should have recognized the pattern immediately. Especially since I worked for days trying to duplicate the same flower for your headpiece and bouquet."

Each woman in the room displayed smiles of approval as Emma put the penny in her left boot and helped Rebecca slip into her new footwear. She lifted her skirt to view her new boots and blinked back tears again. *My father put a lot of thought into this gift.* A knock on the door interrupted. Her father entered hesitantly.

His eyes misty, Charles Muller spoke in a gruff voice. "You look beautiful, Liebling. Your mother would be pleased you wore her dress and veil."

Rebecca blinked rapidly as the tears flowed. "Thank you, Papa."

Charles cleared his throat. "Now, I suppose I must give you away to that cowboy of yours?"

She took her father's extended arm. He patted her hand roughly. "I do approve your choice. Sam is a good man and wants to make you happy. I am even growing used to the idea of being a grandpa to his girls."

Elizabeth opened the door and signaled to the other women. "We best get to our places. We don't want the groom to think you've changed your mind."

Rebecca waited with her father to proceed into the sanctuary.

Sadie and Grace followed Emma down the aisle proudly. They were adorable in matching pink dresses. The girls removed dried rose petals from their baskets and scattered them along their path.

Rebecca trembled as she took the first step. She met Sam's gaze, and her nerves subsided. He looked handsome in his Sunday suit and string tie. His blue eyes seemed to light the room. *His smile is all the encouragement I need.*

Pastor Nelson's voice interrupted her thoughts. "Friends, it is my honor to welcome you. We are gathered here on this day to join in marriage Rebecca Mueller and Sam Brady. Who gives this woman to be married?"

Pastor Nelson gave Rebecca a wink, and she heard other male voices, combined with her father say, "We do."

Rebecca looked at her father whose face tightened before relaxing into a smile. They turned together to see the many men from the town who were an intricate part of her life smile and nod with approval. Doc Benton stood next to Mrs. Doc beaming. Mayor Fears handed his handkerchief to Mr. Young, the blacksmith whose tears were running unashamedly down his cheeks. Friends both old and new joined together to be a part of this special day. Mrs. Potts stood with Lois, surrounded by the girls from her Sunday School class. Her lips quivered as her eyes rested on Molly and Adam who sat on the front row holding their newborn twins.

Emma took her bridal flowers then squeezed her hand briefly as she stood in place beside her as maid of honor. Rebecca's father placed her hand in Sam's, and her heart overflowed. *Thank you, God. I'm so grateful for your provision and love.*

Pastor Nelson took out a handkerchief and wiped tears from his face. "I am often moved with emotion at weddings. But perhaps never quite so early in the ceremony or in such an extreme fashion."

Her father took his seat on the front pew next to Elizabeth and Sara Jane. The pastor encircled the room with his hand. "I believe God used many of you here today to be His extension and thereby you have been a part of what is the perfect example of love. *Agape* is the Greek word for the highest expression of love. It originates from God. It is the pure, self-sacrificing love of God demonstrated by man."

"The Bible teaches us to love our neighbor and our enemies. I sometimes wonder if that's because they are often one and the same." Pastor Nelson laughed at his own joke.

Rebecca smiled when she heard Sam join in with a soft chuckle.

The pastor read 1 Corinthians Chapter 13, before turning his attention to the marriage vows.

Sam's husky voice spoke without prompting. "I, Samuel Paul Brady, take you Rebecca Leah Mueller for my lawful wife, to have and to hold from this day forward for better, for worse, for richer, for poorer, in sickness and health, until death do us part." His hands shook slightly when he placed a gold band on her finger.

At the conclusion of the ceremony, Pastor Nelson once again wiped his face with his handkerchief, his eyes tear-filled. "You may kiss your bride."

After their lips met in their first kiss as man and wife, Rebecca matched Sam's grin.

Pastor Nelson shook Sam's hand. "Congratulations. May God richly bless you." He placed his arm around Rebecca for a brief hug then proclaimed in a loud voice. "Let me introduce for the first time, Mr. and Mrs. Sam Brady."

They left the church to smiling faces and applause. Rebecca felt Sam's hand on the small of her back guide her toward the buggy.

"I figure I'm about the luckiest man in Texas." Sam helped Rebecca into her seat, and they made the short trip to the hotel for the reception.

Rebecca leaned her head on Sam's shoulder. "I think I'm the luckiest woman not only in Texas but the whole world." Her nose twitched, and she sneezed several times in succession. A small feather in the air caught her attention. When they stopped, Rebecca noticed multiple small pieces of fluff floating in the air.

She sneezed again while Sam helped her from the buggy. "I'm sorry honey, I thought I cleaned everything up, but I was in a rush."

Rebecca turned. Soft down danced in the wind. "Sam, are those chicken feathers?"

Sam chuckled. "Yes, but not just any chicken, but rather one you are acquainted with and know by name."

Rebecca put her hand to her mouth and giggled. "Petunia?"

Sam took his hand and brushed a few feathers from his coat. "The one and only. The girls thought their favorite pet ought to be part of the ceremony. They almost got away with it too. I will tell you the whole story some other time. But not today. It's time to go start on our happily ever after."

The End

Kimberly Grist is married to her high school sweetheart, Nelson, who is a pastor in Griffin, Georgia. She and her husband have three adult sons, one with Down syndrome, and she has a passion to encourage others in offering a special needs ministry in the church. Kim is also a grandmother and proud to be a child of the living God. She feels called to help and encourage others and to share experiences both good and bad in order to be the witness that God would have us to be.

Kim has enjoyed writing since she was a young girl, however, began writing her first novel in 2017. Inspired by so many things life has to offer one of which includes her oldest son's diagnosis of cancer she finds it especially gratifying to write a happy ending. "Suffering is, of course, is my least favorite thing. My objective is not to discuss my struggles specifically but to combine a love of history with biblical principles to produce a historical Christian based story that shows how God uses adversity for our good in ways we may never expect."

Social Media:

Facebook: https://www.facebook.com/FaithFunandFriends/

Twitter: https://twitter.com/GristKimberlyAmazon

Author Page: amazon.com/author/kimberlygrist

Website: https://kimberlygrist.com

Other Books by Kimberly Grist

~o0o~

Rebecca's Hope

Raised by her guardian and influenced by the mostly male population of Carrie Town Texas, Rebecca benefited from a forward-thinking, unorthodox education not typical for a young woman in the late Nineteenth century.

As an adult, she is armed with skills that most would covet, yet she lives in a boarding house, works as a waitress and struggles financially. Most single women in the area didn't stay single long. Most, but not her. The one man she had said yes to was dragging his feet. The townspeople all agree she needs a husband. Even the young girls in her Sunday School Class have taken action by writing an ad for the paper.

Wanted: Husband for Rebecca Mueller. **Must be handsome, nice, like children, and live within walking distance of Carrie Town School.

Will her circumstances change and allow her to hold out for true love?

~o0o~

Emma's Dream

In my first novel *Rebecca's Hope*, I introduced a western town in the late 19th century filled with colorful characters and innovative young women. Emma's Dream is a continuation of the tale based on Rebecca's best friend. While other young women in the late nineteenth century are reading about proper housekeeping, Emma studies herd improvement and her cooking skills leave a lot to be desired.

Our story begins several months before Rebecca's wedding. Circumstances require Emma to take on the household chores which include taking care of her six-year-old twin cousins. Like a double-edged sword, help arrives in the form of Grandma Tennessee who manages a household with ease but whose colorful stories, old wives' tales and superstitions flow like a river.

As I researched pioneer life in the late 19th century, I found that superstitions were widely practiced as immigrants migrated and cultures blended. One of my goals as I wrote was to give an accurate account of the period while exposing the inaccuracy of the quotes and beliefs in a humorous way. Hence the birth of the delightful character, Grandma Tennessee.

Emma's Dream is a story of love that's tested by distance and has the perfect combination of history, humor, and romance with an emphasis on faith, friends and good clean fun!

~o0o~

Lois's Risk

Lois Weaver has been schooled to be polite, lady-like, honest, to clean, cook and sew, so that at the proper age she would marry. As an adult, she surpassed her father's expectations with her skills and beauty only to shatter them when she opens a dress shop. She risked everything to start her own business.

Now the handsome bank owner has come calling. So why isn't she happy? And why can't she forget about a certain farmer with big brown eyes? Daniel Lawrence, former Texas Ranger, gained immense satisfaction when he purchased his farm and livestock. His new way of life is not only a means to make a living but adds a sense of fulfillment. The only thing lacking is a wife and family.

He is just shy of proposing when a family tragedy forces him to open his home to his grieving sister and his niece. How could he bring a new wife home to this? Lois is heartbroken because Daniel is ignoring her. Can she go against the 19th-century rules of how a woman should behave and have the courage to tell Daniel how she feels?

Combining history, humor, and romance with an emphasis on faith, friends, and good clean fun, fans of historical romance set in late 19th-century will enjoy *Lois's Risk* a delightful tale of courage and reminds us how God uses adversity to strengthen us and draw us closer to Him.

~o0o~

https://www.amazon.com/dp/B07SM9HKWP

Twenty-year-old Maggie Montgomery, is a

petite young woman ahead of her time. She's had a wonderful childhood and enjoyed spending time with her father and five brothers and is **happiest** working in the smithy with them. A competent cook and housekeeper, as a favor to the local doctor, she moves in to assist his wife who is struggling to recuperate from a bout of pneumonia.

A tomboy at heart, she ignores her mother's pleas to dress more appropriately. Until the son returns. A recent graduate of medical school, although handsome, the young doctor is stoic and obviously put out that his father has hired her to help his mother recuperate. Sparks fly and suddenly for the first time Maggie is concerned more about how she is perceived by others, especially the young doctor? The question is why? Can they get past their first impressions?

Maggie draws on unrelenting strength where iron sharpens iron—forging an unexpected result of the romantic kind.

> **Connect with Kimberly**
> Facebook
> Twitter
> Amazon Author Page
> Website
> Bookbub
> Sign Up for my Newsletter

Made in the USA
Monee, IL
15 June 2022